LUCKY PENNY

SHORT TALES OF MAGICAL REALISM

LUCKY PENNY

SHORT TALES OF MAGICAL REALISM

CONTENTS

1

RITE OF PASSAGE
TIM KELLER

Jackson Harris sat in an ancient wooden office chair both low and wide, yet tall enough that his legs couldn't reach the ground. He liked the creak the chair made as he swung his feet back and forth, but the cop at the desk, the one whose face looked all rolled up like the Sedberry's Shar-Pei, said to "knock it the fuck off."

Jackson glared, but he "knocked it the f—"... He stopped.

Another one walked over. "Hey, big guy, you must be Jackson, right?"

Jackson shifted his glare but said nothing.

"Or Jack; bet they call you Jack, right? Big, strong boy like you... course they do."

Jackson stifled an eye roll. These were cops; they were mean.

"Come on now," the jolly cop said. "No need to be afraid of us; we're the good guys."

Jackson snorted, and then caught himself and blushed—

Mom says it's rude to laugh at people. Why would he be scared of that guy? He looked like a fake blue Santa. He was afraid, though. *What if we didn't get it all? What if she comes back for us?*

"Where's Joey?" he growled tightly.

A shadow eclipsed the whole Santa thing, just for a second, and then passed. "Joey's home with his family," Santa-cop said. "Just like you will be as soon as you answer a few questions."

Another policeman, maneuvering a huge box of doughnuts between the desks, reminded Jackson of how long ago breakfast was. His gaze tracked the box until Santa-cop noticed and smiled, waving Doughnut-cop over. "You think maybe a doughnut would help?"

Jackson nodded like a bobble-head doll.

Doughnut-cop brought him the box and let him choose. "How 'bout a pop?" he asked. "Well, you gotta have something to wash it down, am I right?"

"Yes, sir!" Jackson said. Then, throwing Sharpei-cop a glare, swung his legs like a can-can dancer.

Doughnut-cop handed him a bright red can and popped the tab. "Now, suppose you calm down as best you can and tell us what happened and how the fire started."

Jackson hesitated. No one had believed them, not even their moms and dads, but surely that was because of *her.* Everyone was listening now, weren't they? Besides, the whole Santa thing aside, he was still a cop—and he did have a gun.

"K," he said at last, "but you gotta be careful; Ms. Bair is dangerous."

Santa and doughnut-cop shared a look. Then Santa-cop

got all serious, reached between his legs, and pulled his chair uncomfortably close.

"Oh, we will," he said.

Jackson hesitated, chewed, and drank deep from the can. "First thing is—Water definitely doesn't kill witches. It doesn't melt 'em, or even slow 'em down that much. It just makes them very, very mad. Prob'ly just have to shoot her—"

Santa-cop dropped his doughnut. "Whoa! Wait, you tried to kill her?"

A rumbling belch rolled forth from Jackson like distant thunder. "Mmmhmm," he said at last. Then, wolfing into his second jelly doughnut, "Well, melt her—I don't know if witches can die."

All three cops shared a look. "Maybe you should start at the beginning," Santa-cop said.

Jackson was confused and immediately suspicious. "I did."

"I mean, when... What made you and Joey think Ms. Bair is a witch?"

———

That's me, or was anyway.

Life was pretty good for a kid. I mean, sure, there was the occasional bedtime or television conflict. In general, though, when the worst thing that happens is a two-hour standoff over Brussels sprouts before you can have dessert, existence was pretty charmed—center of the universe ain't bad.

That's how it was for me. Dad would head to work, bossy brothers and sisters to school, and then it was just me and

Mom and a world full to the brim of adventure, TV, and the best snacks in the free world. My little sister's near-pathological need for attention cramped my style somewhat, but nothing I couldn't handle.

Then came my fifth birthday, and the threat of kindergarten loomed large. What a nasty word—kindergarten. All the inconvenience of school and none of the prestige. Still, after numerous promises of lazy days spent coloring, snacking, and napping, I began to relax. And in fairness, I believe to this day that's what Mom thought it would be. Besides, it still seemed so far away. Until suddenly the day arrived.

"Oh dear, let me fix your hair," Mom said, slicking down my cowlick for about the hundredth time that morning.

They were mortal enemies, she and that cowlick, and while it didn't seem to me it would ever be tamed, standing there as she pet me with her spit-slathered hand, I wouldn't be the one to bet against her. Cowlick pasted into submission, Mom took my hand and led me into the school.

"Now you be good, Jackson Harris," she said.

My face fell. This kindergarten thing was really happening. I'd known it would, of course, having watched it happen to my older brothers and sisters, but they had Mrs. Norton. Old Mrs. Norton was everyone's favorite. She'd taught from the basement of her house for decades. The year I came along, however, she retired, leaving the young and pretty Ms. Bair to take over from a hastily cobbled together classroom in the ancient sub-basement of the century-old high school. It was all people had talked about over the summer. Now, it was real.

A pretty lady, much younger than Mom, approached.

"You must be Jackson," she said. "Oh, we're going to have such fun!"

Mom and her talked for a moment, shared a laugh, and then betrayal of betrayal, Mom was leaving—what's more, she seemed happy about it.

"Now, clasp hands, everyone," Ms. Bair said. "Like this." She held my hand in hers for everyone to see.

She led us down some stairs, past the cafeteria, which my brothers called the pit. Down another flight of stairs, through a long hallway, past an old coal shoot and furnace room where great chunks of tubing lay scattered around motorized-looking somethings, the holes to which they connected laid bare. And finally, through a doorway you kind of had to step over to go in.

"Be careful, children," she said. "Always step high so you don't trip."

The room shrieked cheer. Primary colors covered nearly every surface but did little to disguise the industrial nature of the room. Dad said it was an old bomb shelter. The kitchen area for snacks was all steel gray. Next to that, a section of little desks, and at the far end of the room, coat hooks and cubbyholes stood watch over several rugs, "Nap mats," she called them.

The bathrooms were terrifying. The toilet seats operated on a spring. We could sit, but the moment we rose, the seat popped up and the toilets roared like they had a personal score to settle, not only with the contents of the bowl, but with the bearer and his or her progeny and ancestry. Suction pulled at us, even through the rebounding mist of the blast. It was easy to imagine some creature waiting beneath the maw of the drain. One slip, and we'd be gone. It'd happened before, everyone knew, to that one kid, from last year—and he was a high schooler...

We tried everything to keep from flushing. I favored the 'dive from the seat and pull up my big-boy pants from the other side of the door' method. I'm sure others had similar techniques, but some, like Joey, were so scared they tried to hold it all day, which often translated to disastrous results.

Ms. Bair was all smiles when our moms dropped us off. But against the backdrop of the sub-basement, the room, the bathrooms, and the fact that we were surrounded by giants, generally unseen, but definitely not unheard—lunchtime was like being under a stampede—it was clear to us that Ms. Bair didn't smile; she bared her teeth.

The much-vaunted snack time consisted of rabbit food, and story time consisted only of the adventures of Ms. Bair and her magic wand. With it, she could make candy or flowers or even the occasional furry creature appear out of thin air, even do sparks and stuff. Most occurred with a magic word or two, but the thundering command "SILENCE," always accompanied by a blinding flash, never failed to reduce us to quivering blobs of protoplasm. And she was almost never without that wand. Whether weaving tales of her travels in faraway lands, candy, music, lights, or most nefarious of all, naptime—there was that wand and cape.

Like a force of nature, and just as unpredictable, she could make you love her with a word or a touch. Or rain havoc on your life. One day, I was late coming in from tetherball at recess, and she kicked me in the seat in front of everyone. Tears welled up against my will; I couldn't help but take it personally.

I worked extra hard to make up for it, though, tried to go down for my naps, eat all my snacks, anything she needed I volunteered for, snack clean up, erase the board, my hand was always up. Nothing seemed to help.

Anxiety crept beyond the borders of the classroom. My appetite disappeared, nightmares kept me exhausted, and all anyone wanted to talk about was my wonderful new teacher.

"What a sweet lady Ms. Bair is," Mom would say.

I could only nod, when I had to anyway, vowing silently to make her proud. Until one day, during a game of Seven-Up, Ms Bair made fun of me for touching Joey's thumb and told me to pick someone else, in front of everyone.

Shortly thereafter, Joey had an accident trying to avoid the toilets. She hated him, too.

I took solace in the realization that I was not alone.

"Boys," Derek whispered at recess one day. "She hates the boys."

I'd been so busy trying to impress, I hadn't noticed. Now, though, huddled together, talking in low whispers like POW camp conspirators, I saw it was true.

I tried telling Mom I couldn't go back, that I was sick, that the school was scary, the kids were mean, and so was Ms. Bair, but I couldn't explain how. Dad said I should pray and try harder to be good, and to my horror, Mom said she'd talk with Ms. Bair about it.

On vaccination day, I hid. Needles seemed an unnecessary, even cruel addition to my already stressed-out life. There were plenty of places in the industrial graveyard for an enterprising kindergartener to hide, and I loved hide-and-go-seek. I was good at it, too. No match for Ms. Bair, though, she—and to my surprise, my mother—found me in no time. Mom held me down for the shot. I could have gotten away, Dr. Carlisle didn't call me "Tiger" for nothing, but behind my Mom stood Ms. Bair, wand within easy reach.

"You're a miracle worker," Mom said. "He never holds still."

My eyes never left Bair's or that wand.

When Mom left, Ms. Bair berated me in front of everyone for being afraid. This served as a signal to the rest; recess was open season on the victims of her wrath.

"You tattle to your precious mommy again, and I'll turn her into a toad before your very eyes," she hissed, leading us out.

I shuffled around the makeshift playground in a daze. Kimberley Coburn pranced around me and sing-songed, "Scaredy cat, scaredy cat." Even my friends wouldn't venture near.

I blurted, "You'd better shut up!"

My hand flew to my mouth. "Shut up" was forbidden in my house, even more so in class, most especially in regards to Bair's favorite tattletale.

"I'm telling! And Ms. Bair's gonna turn your mom into a toad!" Kimberley said.

So, I punched her.

Her nose burst with a delightful crunch. A siren-wail burbled from her lips, and I drew back again, only to find I couldn't move.

"You little shit!" reverberated across the playground. Next thing I knew, I was at home getting spanked.

"You never hit girls," Dad said.

I tried to explain, but didn't have the words. *They always believed me before.* Mere parents couldn't help anyway, not against magic.

One by one, my friends morphed from allies to collaborators—if a kindergartener can be such a thing—out of cowardice, it seemed. An extra cookie or cone during snack time could have won many over, but Derek? Jamie? Never! Ours was a bond forged in battle, and nothing could have broken it. Nothing ordinary anyway. Ms. Bair's magic reigned supreme.

Only Joey and I could see this had to end. Ms. Bair often left us alone during naptime. Where she went, no one knew, though she'd be gone almost the whole hour. Long after everyone had gone to sleep, I crawled from under my blanket, a prepubescent ninja, avoiding my sleeping classmates like landmines, and crept toward Ms. Bair's desk.

The room was quiet that day, too quiet. There was a forced quality to the sleep noises, and the room seemed rife with slitted eyelids.

Ms. Bair's hand puppets hung impaled en masse on the coat rack. The radio sang softly to itself amid bursts of static. Now and then, the dial flickered faintly like a warning. I reached into her closet and fumbled around until my hand closed around something soft and warm.

Midnight, her cat, exploded spitting and hissing from the darkness. Puppet eyes glared accusingly as I flew back to my nap-mat and under the covers and held my breath until darkness fringed the edges of my vision. No one moved. I couldn't believe my luck.

"Someone was up during nap time," Ms. Bair said upon her return. "Anyone want to own up to it?"

I found the question phenomenally foolish.

"No? Very well," she sighed.

She pulled a large glass ball from her bag, ran her wand over it, and then looked straight at me.

"What makes you think you can go snooping around other people's belongings during nap time? Did you think I wouldn't know?"

I almost fainted, but instead a great swell of righteous rage welled up, and I shouted, "You're mean, and everybody hates you!"

She barked a harsh and nasty laugh. "Just for that, you get to sit in the corner for the movie. And no snacks for anyone this afternoon, courtesy of Jackson Harris." Then softer, "Let's see who they hate now."

The movie was *The Wizard of Oz*, and in spite of my punishment, I watched the whole thing through the mirror by the cubbies. The Oz witches did all the things Bair did and more. The nasty green one could even fly!

Joey and I shared a telepathic glance. *Finally, there's a way.*

Since neither Joey nor I could lift the amount of water we were sure it would take for a witch so vile as Ms. Bair, we needed to bring her to us. The plan was a good one: make sure Kimberly saw us hide in the janitor's closet after recess. The janitor's closet had a hose. It was short and really hard to kink, but together we could manage it. When Kimberley tattled that we were hiding out there after playtime (and there was never any chance she wouldn't), all we had to do was wait.

Then, once Ms. Bair was gone, we'd find all her magic stuff and get rid of it, just in case.

We heard them coming long before their arrival. Hurricane Bair and her acolytes stormed the closet. But we weren't ready, the faucet was too high, and Joey had to step on a bucket to reach it.

The hose was even stiffer than expected, the pressure was so great, it took us both to hold it. The door flew open just as we locked into place. She must have figured it out an instant before we fired. I hope so anyway. Water exploded from the hose so hard, it forced her from the room. We cheered as she fell to the floor and writhed out of range.

But instead of a helpless melting blob, she rose like a dipped cat, sputtering in fury.

Joey and I raced from the room and hid out under the shelf in the old coal shoot. We could see plenty from the inside, plenty being shoes and a bit of thigh. But no one could see in. No one but her. She dragged Joey out kicking and screaming. A crowd of demonic classmates cheered as they followed up the stairs and out into the school yard— I guess it's not so easy to hide from a witch.

I couldn't abandon my friend. I gave chase through the now empty classroom and saw it—prize of prizes—all our plans, my failed attempt during naptime, and there it was— the Holy Grail, the source of the wicked witch's power, sitting out right on her desk.

Touching the magic wand was like touching a living

thing. I gasped and jerked my fingers away. Too late for second thoughts now, it was time to end this. This time, I seized the wand and waded into battle. Power throbbed and pulsed through it, through me. That's when I knew for certain: Ms. Bair really could change us into toads. Who knew how far she could go with this thing in her possession?

Hushed whispers morphed to shouts of glee. Shackles of fear dropped away— liberator, warrior, avenger—friendships renewed with the merest appreciative glance. Her acolytes parted before me like the Red Sea, then fell in behind as I went.

"Ms. Bair," Kimberly shrieked, "it's Jackson and he has—"

"SILENCE!" My command struck Kimberly dumb, as thunder reverberated across the playground.

Bair stopped in her tracks and turned slowly. "Just what do you think you're doing?"

"Let him go!" I said.

She smiled. "Don't be foolish, child."

"Let him go!"

She dropped Joey, who landed so hard I heard the wet thump. "Satisfied?"

"Now I turn *you* into a toad!" I yelled and swung for the cheap seats.

Bair just cackled, and to my mounting horror, remained decidedly un-toad-like.

Throughout the chase, the crystal at the end of the wand had burned with righteous fire. Now, as I looked down, I saw something that looked a lot like a plastic toy with a burned-out light bulb.

Ms Bair stepped forward and grabbed it. "Give me that, you little shit!"

And I almost did, but Joey dove at her leg and latched on with his teeth. She kicked him pretty good and was turning back to me when I swung at her head. That's when things got confusing. Blood shot from a cut above her eye, and an inhuman snarl issued from her lips as she charged.

I shrieked a stream of unintelligible noise, and wish or command, defense, offense, or all of the above, a blinding flash shot from the wand. And Ms Bair, the wicked witch of Franklin County School District Kindergarten, collapsed, while the school exploded behind her. Well, the kindergarten entrance part, anyway. When I looked back, she was gone.

"Old wiring in the furnace," they said. Lucky we weren't in the building when it happened. Only we knew the truth.

Off we went to Mrs. Norton's while the school was repaired. Turns out, Mrs. Norton was a big fan of lazy days spent coloring, snacking, and napping. And was never, ever mean.

The cops were pretty steamed about the whole attempted murder thing.

But no charges; we were kindergarteners after all. Ms. Bair disappeared, her belongings, creepy puppets included, burned in the fire. And no one could find her, Midnight, the crystal ball, or the mysterious wand.

I've taken very good care of it over the years. And every now and again, when life gets hard, I think I still see a spark of magic in the plastic bulb on the end.

THE KITCHEN RUG

L.S. KUNZ

Sharon hauled two-year-old Chrissy into one arm and two bags of groceries into the other. She could have made two trips into the house in half the time but didn't realize it till halfway up the driveway, arms trembling, eggs teetering, and Chrissy yanking at her hair.

At the front door, Sharon shifted Chrissy higher up on her hip, wrenched the doorknob with two fingers, caught a falling loaf of French bread with her chin, and pushed the door wide with her foot.

The family room was so dark only silhouettes were visible. The red glow of the setting sun cast a Martian tinge over the matching furniture set. No one had bothered to turn on a lamp. Of course they hadn't. They'd forget to dress themselves if Sharon didn't remind them.

Still, their idleness had its benefits. In the dim orange haze, the upholstery didn't look so worn and the clutter receded into shadow.

Sharon staggered over the threshold and kicked the door shut behind her. When the door slammed, Ted twitched in his sleep. Not even eight o'clock yet, but Ted was already dozing in his recliner. His stockinged feet dangled off the end of the footrest like two dead trout. Blurry images from the TV danced across the thick lenses of his glasses.

Isabella lounged nearby on the couch, her lanky legs splayed over the armrest, her toenails painted a garish red that screamed bawdy even in the bad light. With one hand on the remote and the other elbow deep in a bag of potato chips, Isabella looked like she might be in for the evening. That would be a relief.

"No date tonight?"

Isabella clicked the remote. The TV screen switched from a sequined rock star flanked by scantily clad dancers to the news. Isabella grimaced and clicked back to the music video.

"Steve's picking me up at eight."

Steve. The name turned Sharon's blood up to boil. All swagger and hair product, Steve was a dead ringer for Ted nineteen years ago. But Isabella wouldn't make the same mistakes she had. She wouldn't let her.

Halfway to the kitchen, Sharon tripped on a scattered mess of toys and electronics and, Sharon squinted, were those pieces of the toaster?

"Mike!" Sharon shouted at the door to the basement. "Come clean up this mess!"

No answer.

"Don't you ignore me!"

Chrissy whimpered and slapped Sharon's chin with a pudgy hand.

"Oh, sweetie," Sharon softened her voice and pressed a cheek to Chrissy's tousled curls. "It's okay. Don't cry."

Then she turned back to the stairs and bellowed, "Michael T. Burrows, get your scrawny butt up here and clean up your toys!"

"Just a minute!" came a distracted voice from the basement.

"I'm not asking. If these toys aren't cleaned up in 30 seconds, they're going in the trash!"

"Fine!"

A rumble of footsteps preceded the angry blur that was Sharon's middle child.

Sharon didn't bother to say hello. Mike didn't have time to talk. Not with his buddies in the basement and a video game on pause.

In the kitchen, Sharon flicked the light switch with an elbow, then leaned one way to dump the groceries on the counter and the other way to let a squirming Chrissy slide to the floor.

"Go say hi to Daddy, sweetie."

Sharon gave her toddler a push in the right direction, then pulled two bunches of bananas from a grocery sack. It seemed like way too many bananas, but since Mike had turned thirteen, he had stopped chewing food and started inhaling it. He was like one of the insects they talked about on TV who eat their weight in food every day. He was like locusts. A plague of locusts.

Sharon set the bananas in the fruit bowl and called into the family room. "Isabella, come help put the groceries away."

"In a minute." Isabella switched the TV station.

"Now, please."

Isabella sighed. "All right."

As Chrissy toddled out of the kitchen, Isabella shambled in—long legs, glorious thigh gap, tousled mane, button lips painted glossy red to match her toes.

Sharon blinked. When had little Isabella Burrows become a bombshell?

"Isn't it too cool out for shorts? It's only May."

Isabella shrugged and turned to cram a head of lettuce into the vegetable crisper. "It's almost June."

Sharon eyed her daughter's backside. "It's time to toss those shorts anyway. They're getting worn in the seat."

Isabella glanced over her shoulder at her own rump. "I like them this way."

In the family room, Chrissy reached her pudgy arms toward Ted. "Up."

No response from the recliner.

"Da-Da. Up."

"Ted," said Sharon from the kitchen. "Your daughter wants you."

Ted snorted in his sleep and shifted position.

Sharon carried crackers and bread into the unlit pantry and groped for the light switch. "Have you finished your college applications yet?"

Isabella loaded yogurt cups into the fridge. "I decided not to do them."

Sharon's finger found the switch but didn't turn it on. "Why not?"

"I'm not going to college."

Sharon blinked. Unbidden, an image of herself nineteen years ago flashed into her mind. She had been so young then. Barely eighteen herself. So many dreams—college, travel, fame, fortune. Had she been a bombshell? Maybe. There hadn't been time to find out. Her thigh gap had disappeared not long after the night Ted coaxed her into the backseat of his Buick.

In the dark pantry, a salad bar of emotions spread out before Sharon—fear, anger, resentment, disbelief. She didn't peruse the options, though. No time to indulge.

Leaving the lights off, she deposited the bread and crackers on the shelf, worked her face into the shape of mild interest, and walked back out into the light of the kitchen. "What do you mean? You've always talked about college."

Isabella pulled a sack of apples from the bag. "Steve and I decided I don't need a degree. It would be a waste of money."

Sharon longed to retreat back into the dark pantry and gorge herself at her salad bar of self-pity, but she stayed put. "What's Steve got to do with it?"

Isabella toppled the apples into the fruit bin. "I'm going to work while Steve earns his degree. That way, he can get a good job and I can stay home with the kids."

Sharon gripped the back of the nearest barstool. She needed something solid to hold onto. "Kids? You've got the rest of your life to have kids. You're only eighteen."

Isabella shrugged and toppled oranges into the bin on top of the apples. "You were eighteen when you got married."

"Yeah, but...." Sharon stopped.

She had been about to say that getting married was the

worst mistake of her life. But there was her groom in the next room, and here was the daughter that had forced the shotgun wedding. She couldn't speak those words. Not ever.

She changed course. "What about all your plans?"

Isabella looked genuinely puzzled. "What plans?"

"To travel." Sharon searched Isabella's face. "You know, London, Paris, New York."

Isabella shook her head. "I don't know what you're talking about."

Sharon gripped the chairback harder. "Don't you remember? When you were little? You'd sit there on the kitchen rug and pretend it was a magic carpet."

Sharon blinked at the ratty rug, threadbare after nineteen years of shoes and stains and spills. She had tread on it every day of her married life. When had she last noticed it?

"You sat there while I folded laundry and told me all the places you'd visit when you grew up—Cairo, Istanbul, Hong Kong."

Isabella smiled. "Oh, yeah. I remember. I thought it was magic because the tag said it was made in Turkey."

"That's right," said Sharon. The rug *had* looked magic back then. Woolen threads of maroon and gold weaved into exotic designs from faraway places. She had never really thought about it. Who had time with earaches and errands and mouths to feed?

She had only ever seen the rug as the outrageously useless wedding gift it was. She never had figured out what Mom had been thinking. Let's see. What should I give to my eighteen-year-old, eight-months pregnant daughter at her shotgun wedding? A microwave? No. A laundry basket? No. I know, a handmade rug from Turkey.

Isabella shoved celery into the crisper. "That was pretend. Flying carpets aren't real."

"But London and Paris are. Airplanes can take you there anytime you like."

Isabella shrugged. "Why? Steve's here."

Out on the street, a car horn blared twice.

Isabella plopped the carton of milk she had been holding back onto the counter. "That's Steve."

Sharon opened her mouth. Not sure her voice would work. "At least put the milk away."

Isabella didn't even glance back. "Steve said not to be late. He has a surprise planned."

"Be home by ten. It's a school night."

Isabella groaned. "It's the last week of school. Tonight hardly counts as a school night."

"It counts," retorted Sharon as Isabella breezed out of the kitchen. "Be home by ten."

In the living room, Isabella tousled Chrissy's wispy pigtails and tossed a spaghetti-string clutch over her shoulder.

"Bye, Dad," she said to the recliner and disappeared out the front door.

For an instant, there was silence. Then Chrissy let out a long wail. "Uuuuup, Da-Da!"

"For crying out loud." Sharon stormed into the family room. "Ted!"

Ted blinked awake and smiled. "Hello, beautiful."

Sharon pointed at the now red-faced Chrissy. "Would you please pick up your daughter?"

Ted held out his arms, and Chrissy flopped into them. As Ted swooped his youngest into his lap, Sharon turned back to the kitchen only to trip over a now neatly stacked pile of toys and the remains from what had definitely been the toaster.

Sharon kicked the pile, sending toys and toaster parts skittering across the carpet. One hit the wall with a smack.

Chrissy sobbed.

"What's wrong, Hon?" Ted nestled Chrissy into his chest and switched to his daddy voice. "Just look at the mess Mommy made."

Chrissy giggled.

Sharon squeezed her fists till her fingers bit into her palms. Maybe if she drew blood she could go to the hospital. Anything to escape this house. This ... this prison.

"Just put Chrissy to bed, will you?"

"Is it your bedtime, Chrissy-poo?"

Chrissy squealed. Sharon didn't have to turn to see he was tickling her. Sharon's insides churned. He was as bad as the kids. Why couldn't he just do what she said?

"Ted!"

"We're going. We're going."

Ted dragged his tall, lanky frame from the recliner and scooped Chrissy onto his back. He departed the family room at a gallop, Chrissy bouncing and giggling with every step. Sharon fumed. Why did he have to get Chrissy all riled up? At this rate, she would never get to sleep.

Back in the kitchen, Sharon stared at the half-empty bags of groceries. The carton of milk on the counter. How had her life come to this? Thirty-seven years old and nothing to show for it. No degree. No stamps in her passport. No passport. Just three kids, one of whom could very well climb into the bed of Steve's Chevy tonight and start the whole pathetic cycle over again.

Sharon tried to lift the milk carton. But it was too heavy. Life was too heavy. She couldn't heft it one more day. She sank onto the rug beneath her feet and ran her hand across the rough wool. Despite years of neglect, flecks of gold still shone through.

Brushing away a cornflake, she traced her finger along a faded flourish. If only it really were magic and could whisk her away from the nightmare that had become her life. No kids. No Ted. No responsibilities. She could go anywhere, do anything, and never, ever look back.

Leaning across the rug, she flipped up the edge. There it was—barely legible now—"Handmade in Turkey." Just seeing the tag took her back.

"Turkey, Mommy. See? It's a *magic* carpet. Where should we go? Paris?"

Day after day, Isabella had traveled the world on this rug. And Sharon had folded laundry. Endless baskets of laundry. Why hadn't she set the clothes aside and joined Isabella on the rug? If she had, maybe Isabella would be planning a graduation trip now instead of a wedding. How could she throw everything away? And for what? A stupid boy who would wind up in a faux leather recliner of his own in a few years.

Sharon looked at the hand clasping the edge of the rug. Could it possibly be hers? It was so worn, so tired, so...unaccomplished. It had never lifted a glass of wine in Rome or gripped a stone on the Great Wall. It had never done anything but change diapers and scrub toilets. It was the hand of a stranger. A stranger she didn't want to know.

Tears welled in her eyes. She squeezed her eyelids shut, but one tear escaped, slid down her cheek, dripped from her chin, and landed with a splash on the rug.

Warmth radiated out from the wet spot and spread across the rug. Sharon sensed it in her fingertips. At first, it seemed like just the warmth from her hand, but the temperature rose till the whole rug felt as fluffy and warm as towels fresh from the dryer.

Sharon ran her hand across the wool, letting the toasty fibers prickle her palm.

All at once, the rug shifted, knocking Sharon from her knees to her behind.

The rug shuddered and stretched like a dog waking from a long, lazy slumber. Sharon planted her hands behind her for support.

Then, in one swift motion, the rug lifted straight up off the linoleum. The move was so sudden, it left Sharon's stomach behind. She gasped like a schoolgirl on a Ferris wheel and peeked over the edge at the dirty dishes in the sink. The rug felt solid and steady as the floor, but there was no floor beneath her. Nothing but air.

She knew she should be scared. But she wasn't. Somehow it felt right. Like coming home. She wrapped her fingers around the side of the rug, leaned toward the open kitchen window, and said, "Let's go."

The rug went.

It wedged through the open window and glided down the sleepy street, coasting in and out of lamplight past one suburban house after another. All the houses blended together—an endless line of lawns, satellite dishes, and mini-vans. Sharon had driven by these houses every day for, what, twelve years? But it was as if she had never seen them before. She couldn't distinguish one from the next. From this new vantage point, they all looked the same.

The rug reached a stop sign and stopped, throwing Sharon off balance. For a long moment, the rug hovered there. Its ragged fringe fluttered in the light breeze.

Out of habit, Sharon looked right and left. But the rug had other plans. Without warning, it launched straight up into the sky. Helpless against the thrust, Sharon fell to her back. Above her, the spring moon—round as a saucer—shone down on her like a spotlight, and the stars leaped toward her like in the space travel shows Mike liked to watch after school. What did he call it? Hyper-warp? Super worm-hole shortcut?

The air grew thin and downright chilly. Sharon's skin goose-pimpled, but she didn't care. The rug stopped abruptly. Sharon's body rose right up off the rug and hovered in midair. Her stomach churned. She wanted to scream. Then she plopped safely back down on the rug.

Clinging to the fringe, she leaned over the edge. She couldn't see her house anymore. Or her street. Or her neigh-borhood. Just twinkling lights. The lights below blended with the stars above so that she could no longer tell where Earth ended and the sky began.

Letting go of the fringe, she spread her arms wide and breathed deeply. It felt like her first breath in nineteen years. Beneath her, the rug shuddered and stretched as if it, too, could finally breathe. Then it shot forward, knocking Sharon back on her hands.

The rug glided and dipped and twirled as if it would dance in the wind forever. But eventually a dip deepened and the rug dove in roller-coaster drops toward a sea of lights below.

The closer the skyline drew, the more familiar it became. New York City. Finally, the rug drifted up Fifth Avenue and circled the glowing spire of the Empire State Building before coasting out into New York Harbor, where it circumnavigated the Statue of Liberty's gleaming crown and spiraled up her arm, around her flaming torch, and away.

Then it was off to London and Paris, where Sharon startled the beady-eyed ravens at the Tower of London before coasting across the Thames in the winsome glow of Tower Bridge, over the ghostly white cliffs of Dover, and across the English Channel to touch the tip of the Eiffel Tower with one extended finger.

The rug lingered in Venice, gliding up one quiet canal and down another. No one seemed to mind. A sleepy gondolier winked when he saw Sharon and broke into song.

In Rome, the rug circled the Colosseum's pocked arcades and glided right into the Pantheon only to cause a small ruckus when it rose straight up into the great dome and out the oculus into silver moonlight. It paused at Trevi Fountain's flowing waters for Sharon to toss a coin over her left shoulder. Then it was off again.

In Istanbul, the rug buzzed the Blue Mosque before drifting into the spice bazaar. As the rug meandered up one crowded aisle and down another, vendors of vibrant teas and spices stopped bartering to stare. The rug showed no concern. It just bobbed as if to say hello. Sharon felt as at home as the rug, breathing in the pungent scent of cinnamon and saffron. She even reached down and snatched a taste of Turkish Delight from the fingertips of a startled tourist.

Sharon hardly recognized herself. The Sharon she knew would never steal, especially not a sample from the hand of a stranger. But this Sharon took the morsel with a wink and a smile and popped it into her mouth, where it melted on her tongue like sugary gold.

North of Beijing, the rug snaked along the Great Wall, down through dark forest and up steep peaks, before it ducked back into the Forbidden City, where it wandered among the imperial courts and palaces. Then south, over Angkor Wat's ancient spires and Bangkok's reclining Buddha.

The rug sped up when it reached the Pacific, its fringe fluttering in the salty breeze. Across the long ocean, Sharon tried to stay awake. She sensed that they had gone as far as they could and the rug was returning home. Eyes bleary, she woke once to see a hot, orange river of lava inching into tropical forest. Hawaii? Her eyes slipped shut again.

When she woke again, she was in her own bed. Ted snored softly beside her.

She blinked, looked around the dingy white walls with crooked prints of faraway places, and sighed. What a wonderful dream. If only she could have stayed on the kitchen rug forever. There were so many adventures yet to have—north to see polar bears and fjords, glaciers and aurora borealis; south to see penguins and Iguazu, the Southern Cross and Easter Island; east to Kilimanjaro and Everest, Fiji and Cairo, to see lions and elephants, koala bears and kangaroos. Having tasted the world, how could she stop now?

She glanced at the clock. Six-thirty. She had slept in. She needed to coax Isabella and Mike out of bed to get ready for school. Chrissy would wake up any minute and want to play. Ted would want scrambled eggs before work.

She dragged herself from bed, clinging to the feeling of wind in her hair, the scent of sea breeze that lingered in her nostrils.

In the kitchen, she found the half-empty grocery bags where she had left them. The milk carton was there, too, where Isabella had abandoned it. But it was empty now beside an empty bag of cookies. Mike and his buddies.

The kitchen rug was where it should be, as old and stained and ordinary as ever. Sharon squatted down to give it a loving rub. Her hand ran over some crumbs. Mike again. He and his friends never did eat over plates. But when she swept the crumbs into her palm, it wasn't cookies. It was.... No, it couldn't be. Could it? Sharon slipped a crumb into her mouth and felt the sweet taste of sugary gold on her tongue. Turkish Delight.

A slow smile spread across Sharon's face. She looked down at the rug. At freedom. At all her dreams come true. She could leave tonight and never come back. She could climb the Matterhorn, circle Neuschwanstein, buzz Red Square. She could run with the gazelles, cruise the Amazon, migrate with the whales. She could....

A whimper floated up the hall. Sharon blinked, clearing the stars from her eyes. Chrissy was awake. Right on schedule. Three, two, one. Sharon ticked off the seconds with her finger. On one, the shower started. Sharon held her breath, and there it was, right on cue—Ted belting out La Traviata in the shower as if he were on stage at Carnegie Hall.

It was the soundtrack of Sharon's life. The sounds that signaled a new day in the same old life. But this morning, Chrissy's cry didn't pierce her eardrums, and Ted's operatic offerings didn't make her want to soap up the shower floor before he stepped onto his steamy stage.

It was sweet. Charming really—her family's first breaths in the new day. Ted was happy, and Chrissy wanted her mommy.

"Mom?"

Sharon looked up to see a chagrined Mike in the kitchen doorway. He was holding the toaster—completely reassembled. It looked like new, as if its insides had never been scattered across the living room floor.

Mike held the toaster out like a peace offering. "I'm sorry I took the toaster apart. I just wanted to see how it worked."

Sharon's heart swelled as if to burst. She stood up and pulled her son and her toaster into a tight hug. "I'm sorry I yelled. I was just so tired last night."

With her son in her arms, Sharon saw her kitchen as if for the first time. She wasn't trapped here. She never had been. She had chosen to climb into the backseat of Ted's

Buick, and she had chosen to stay all these years. Just like Isabella, she didn't need a magic carpet to leave. There were airplanes available anytime to take her anywhere she wanted to go.

Sharon tousled Mike's hair. She hadn't needed the rug any more than her mom had.

Mike squirmed out of her embrace.

"We need more milk," he said as he deposited the toaster on the counter and headed for the fridge.

Sharon stooped down, kissed the tips of her fingers, and pressed them to the rug.

"Thank you," she whispered.

She brushed her hand across the rug. Beneath years of dust, a flourish of gold glittered. She gathered the rug around her in a hug. It felt like her mom's arms enveloping her. Outside, she shook the rug till all the dust blew away and it shone once more.

Then, slowly, she folded the rug in half and in half twice more and draped it over her arm. With the dust gone, it smelled of spice and the sea.

She walked down the hall to Isabella's door and entered after a peremptory knock. The first thing she saw was her little girl's long legs tangled up in rumpled blankets. The second thing she saw was the thin gold band on her little girl's finger.

Her heartbeat slowed. She blinked to keep from blacking out. That couldn't be what it looked like. Could it?

Sharon sat on the edge of the bed and smoothed the blankets. Isabella blinked her brown eyes open, smiled, and held out her hand, showing off the speck of a diamond.

Tears leapt to Sharon's eyes. She wiped them away.

Isabella grinned. "I'm engaged."

Sharon grasped Isabella's hand and gazed into her eyes, looking for any hint of doubt. "You haven't even graduated high school yet. Are you sure this is what you want?"

Isabella rolled her eyes. "I graduate next week, Mom. I'm not a kid anymore. You can't stop me from getting married."

Sharon smiled. With surprise, she realized the smile was genuine.

"It's not what I wanted for you. But if this is what you want, I won't stand in your way."

Suspicious, Isabella raised an eyebrow. "You're not going to yell? Or cry? I thought you would lose your mind for sure."

Sharon sniffled back more tears. "No, dear. I'm happy for you."

Isabella yanked her hand back as if Sharon might bite. "But what about all that talk last night about Paris and Cairo and Istanbul? You're not disappointed?"

"Of course, I hoped you would go to college and see the world and do all the things I never did. But you have to follow your own dreams, not mine."

Isabella didn't look convinced.

Sharon looked down and remembered the kitchen rug clutched to her chest. "Look," she said, "I even have an engagement present for you."

She held the rug up, wincing as she did. She could have sworn it made a ripping noise as it tore away from her heart. She pressed the rug into her daughter's arms. The gesture triggered a memory of her own mom pressing the rug into her arms.

She said the same words to Isabella that her mother had said to her. "I never needed this, darling. I hope you don't either, but it's yours all the same."

Isabella flipped the fabric over and raised an eyebrow. "Isn't this the kitchen rug?"

Sharon smiled. "Something like that."

Then she stood and walked back to the dirty dishes.

3

WHERE THE MOUNTAIN WAITS
KATIA COMBE

The wooden door creaks as I push it open, the sound sharp against the hush of the morning. A bell above the frame jingles a soft, almost apologetic chime. I step inside and pause, my eyes adjusting to the dim light. The scent hits me first: old paper, beeswax polish, and something earthy, like dried coca leaves.

"Buenos días," I say, my voice barely above a whisper.

From behind a desk cluttered with index cards and a chipped ceramic mug, an older man looks up. His glasses slide down his nose as he squints at me. "Buscas algo en especial?"

I pause. My Spanish is too rusty for the kind of question I want to ask, so I answer in English. "I'm looking for Inca stories. The kind passed down through generations. Like bedtime stories."

He smiles, slow and knowing. He switches languages without missing a beat. "Ah. Then you'll want the back room.

Past the Quechua dictionaries. There's a shelf that doesn't get many visitors."

I thank him and walk deeper into the bookstore. The floorboards groan beneath my boots, and the air grows cooler. I trail my fingers along the spines as I walk. A shaft of sunlight filters through a high window, catching motes of dust dancing in the air.

The back room is smaller, more intimate. The walls are lined with mismatched shelves, and a woven tapestry hangs crookedly above a reading chair. My fingertips tingle in anticipation of opening a book.

I scan the nearest shelf. A slim red book speaks to me, tucked between two thick volumes on agricultural rites. Its cover is embroidered with a golden sunburst, faded but still radiant. I pull it free, and the fabric is warm, as if it's been waiting.

I open it. The pages are soft, almost velvety. The ink is dark brown, handwritten in looping script. Spanish and Quechua mingle like old friends. I whisper the first line aloud: "Ñuqaqa kaypi kani."

"I am here," I whisper.

Behind me, the floor creaks.

"You found it," says the Bookkeeper.

I turn. He stands in the doorway, arms folded, eyes heavy with something I can't name. Sadness?

"What is it?" I ask.

He steps forward, slowly. "A book of truths. Stories passed down by those who listened to the mountains. It chooses who reads it."

I glance down at the illustration in the book, two peaks

side by side. The taller one is labeled Huayna Picchu, the other Machu Picchu. I trace the names with my finger, whispering them aloud.

"Machu Picchu," I say.

The Bookkeeper nods. "From Quechua. Machu means 'old,' Picchu means 'peak.'"

"And Huayna Picchu?"

"Huayna means 'young.' So—'young mountain.'"

I smile, amused by the contrast. "So the old and the young, side by side."

He doesn't smile back. "Yes. And the young one is the one that takes."

I pause. "Takes what?"

He looks at me. "Huayna Picchu is not only young, señorita. He is proud. Too proud to let thousands walk on him without payment. Every step drains him, just a little. His breath, his strength. So, every ten years, he comes to collect."

I blink. "Collect what?"

He shrugs. "No one speaks of it. All we know is that something is taken."

I laugh softly. "Sounds like a myth to keep hikers humble."

He smiles softly.

"I'll take it," I say.

He bows his head in reverence. A shiver runs down my spine. I pay for the book and leave without looking back.

I came to Peru to honor my mother. She died last spring. She used to tell me stories of her homeland: of mountains that breathed, of hummingbirds that carried messages from the dead, of flowers that bloomed only when spoken to kindly. I have no family left, just her voice in my memory, and this trail.

The next day, the van rattles to a stop at KM 82. I step out into the crisp morning air. The mountains loom like guardians, mist curling around their shoulders.

A man in a red windbreaker waves us over. He's tall, with a sun-worn face and warm eyes.

"Buenos días," he says. "I'm Mateo, your guide for the next several days. There will be steep climbs, cold nights, and moments that test you. But if you listen, if you really listen, the trail will speak."

I nod, unsure if he means metaphorically or not.

Mateo gestures toward the group. "Take a moment and meet each other."

I glance around. There's a couple from Canada, a solo hiker with headphones, two older women laughing softly. And then there's me. Standing still. My eyes go to the peaks. They really look like people. I smile. If I were a mountain, what would I think about?

Mateo walks past me and says quietly, "You feel it, don't you?"

I turn. "Feel what?"

He smiles, but it's not playful. "The invitation." And he walks away.

I don't answer. That was strange. Maybe living in the mountains makes people act weird. I shrug and go back to the view. The air smells like eucalyptus and dust. It's beautiful here. I can't imagine things have changed much since the Inca times.

"Let's go," Mateo says, and we start walking.

My boots crunch over the gravel at KM 82. I glance back once before stepping onto the Inca Trail. My skin prickles. I feel like I'm walking into a portal. I giggle. If I were a fairy, I'd live here.

I hike in silence, letting my breath sync with the sway of my pack. Around midday, I pause to drink water near a bend in the trail. A hummingbird, emerald and gold, hovers inches from my face.

I freeze. It flutters, then lands on my shoulder. I feel its tiny heartbeat against my collarbone. Then it's gone.

"Did you see that?" I ask a porter nearby.

He stares at me, then mutters, "La montaña te mira."

I blink. "The mountain is watching me? What does that mean?"

But he's already walking away.

That evening, after dinner, I open the book. I read about sacred animals that guard the Inca trail. One is the emerald and gold hummingbird. There's a picture. My pulse quickens.

"I saw that," I say to one of the elderly ladies.

"You did? How lucky. I didn't see any hummingbirds." She turns back to her friend.

I smile, happiness bursting in me. I flip through the book, sacred flowers, foxes, condors. All tributes to Mother Earth.

"Get a good night's rest. We will see you tomorrow," Mateo says.

I walk to my campsite and lay on my sleeping bag, no tent tonight. Stars bloom overhead, slowly at first, then all at once. The Milky Way stretches like a river of light. I find the Southern Cross, Mama Quilla's eyes, and the shadow of the dark llama. The wind threads through the grass. A night bird calls. The silence wraps around me like a woven shawl, and I fall asleep.

I dream of a woman standing between two peaks. Her dress is woven with gold thread and feathers, her face painted with ash and light. She doesn't speak, just looks at me like she knows me.

"*Ñuqaqa kaypi kani.*"

I wake with my heart pounding and a strange warmth in my chest. Not fear. Something else. Curiosity, maybe.

She says, *I am here.* I shake my head, trying to clear it. The dream clings to me, too vivid, too real. I yawn. My imagination must be working overtime. I roll over and drift back into sleep.

The next morning, we begin to climb. It's brutal. My legs ache, my breath comes in short bursts, and the altitude presses against my chest like a stone. The trail narrows, winding between jagged rocks and patches of scrub. Mist curls around the peaks, and the silence feels thick.

I look down and notice purple, orange, and red wildflowers along the trail. I kneel. Their petals are warm, almost pulsing. The same flowers from my book. I smile. This place is wonderful.

Mateo walks beside me, his pace steady. "This is the highest point of the trail," he says. "Warmiwañusqa. Dead Woman's Pass."

I glance up. The silhouette of the mountain does look like a woman lying down. Her arms folded, face turned skyward.

"Why is it called that?" I ask.

He shrugs. "Some say it's the shape. Others say it's where the mountain listens most closely."

I smile. Everything here has a story, the animals, the plants, even the stones. I feel blessed to be here, to witness this beauty. Grateful that it's been preserved, that people like me can still walk these sacred paths.

As we reach the summit, the wind picks up. I stop and pull out my windbreaker. The wind whistles around me, almost like it's trying to speak.

"Clara."

I freeze.

"Clara"

My name is whispered in the wind.

"Did you hear that?" I ask Mateo.

He looks at me, eyes unreadable. "You okay?"

"Um," I strain my ears, but there is only the wind. I shrug. "I think I'm just tired."

"Make sure you drink plenty of water. Altitude sickness is no joke."

I nod, and he moves away to check on the rest of the group. That was strange. I pull out my water bottle and take a long sip. Definitely don't want to get altitude sickness.

I look out over the valley. Wow, it's stunning. How have the Peruvians kept this land so pure, so untouched by the outside world?

"Let's get going; we're almost to camp," Mateo says.

It takes us another hour of hiking, but we make it.

I sit cross-legged on the woven mat, my legs aching in that good, earned way. The stars are still absent, and the sky shifts to a muted lavender. Steam curls from my bowl of quinoa soup. I cradle it in both hands, letting the warmth seep into my fingers. The broth is earthy, flecked with bits of potato and wild herbs. I take a slow sip. It tastes like the trail, and I smile.

Around me, the others murmur in Spanish and Quechua, laughter flickering like firelight. I catch snippets, someone's boots fell apart, someone else saw a condor. I smile, but I don't speak.

A plate of trout lands beside me, glistening with mushroom sauce. I tear off a piece of bread, Pan Chuta, thick and sweet. I dip it into the sauce. The flavors bloom in my mouth: smoky, tender, alive. I chew slowly, watching the cook ladle soup into another bowl with the grace of someone who's done this a thousand times.

I glance at the mountains. They're dark now, hulking silhouettes against the fading sky. I feel small. But not in a bad way.

The rest of the evening goes fast, and I decide to turn in. I walk to my camp, and I stop in my tracks. A fox stands in front of my tent. Its yellow eyes stare into mine. It blinks, then spits a small stone toward me and walks away.

"Did that just happen?"

I glance around, making sure the fox isn't lingering. I pick up the stone, and it's smooth, shaped like a sunburst. My eyes widen. I've seen this before. I pull out the journal. There it is: a hand-drawn picture. Same shape. Same mark. Labeled *Inti's mark.*

I roll the stone in my hand. Coincidence? Maybe. I slip it into my pocket and crawl into my sleeping bag.

Sleep comes quickly, and she's waiting for me.

The woman in the ceremonial Incan dress stands in a field of golden grass, arms open, face radiant. Behind her, the mountains rise, not as ruins, but as living temples. Machu Picchu glows in the morning light, untouched by time. I see farmers tending terraces, children chasing llamas, women weaving by their homes. The land breathes with them. They don't just live on it. They are part of it. She takes my hand, warm and steady, and places it gently on the earth.

At first, I feel only the coolness of stone. But then, beneath my palm, a pulse. Slow. Rhythmic. Alive.

I gasp. It's not imagined. The land is breathing.

A warmth spreads through my fingers, up my arm, into my chest. My heart stumbles, then steadies, syncing with the rhythm beneath me. My skin tingles. My throat tightens. Tears rise without warning.

The earth hums with something ancient, something tender. It's not just life. It's love. Fierce, quiet, unconditional.

I press my hand deeper into the soil, as if I could anchor myself there forever. My jaw unclenches. The ache I've carried in my heart. The grief, longing, and loneliness begin to diminish.

I am being held.

Not by the woman. Not even by the mountain.

By the land itself.

My breath stutters in my chest. A warmth blooms behind my eyes, blurring everything. My lips part, stretching into a wide smile. My shoulders loosen, my fingers tingle. It's like sunlight spilling through me, chasing out the shadows.

Joy. Real joy.

When I wake, the feeling lingers. I smile again, softer this time. My mom was right. This land is magical.

The next day we begin the hike toward Wiñay Wayna, and everything feels different. The air is softer. The stones beneath my boots seem to hum, and I gasp at a small waterfall hidden in the foliage. Butterflies in yellow, blue, and white flit around me. One lands on my shirt, its wings opening and closing like a heartbeat.

Mateo notices. "They follow you," he says.

I smile. "Maybe they think I'm one of them."

He doesn't laugh. Just smiles a small smile and walks ahead.

We near the ruins of Runkurakay around midday, and I pause to catch my breath. The air is thin, and from the corner of my eye I see a llama.

Alone.

It emerges from the jungle like some shaggy oracle, its gait slow and deliberate, as if it's been summoned. It stops a few feet from me and stares. It's soft. Intentional. Its ears twitch. Then, with surprising grace, it bows its head.

I blink.

I glance around. No one else in sight. Just me, the ruins, and this solemn, slightly lopsided creature. I don't know why, but I kneel, unsure whether I'm about to commune with an ancient spirit or pet a very spiritual farm animal. Slowly, reverently, I place my hand on its forehead.

The moment stretches.

A pulse, gentle and steady, flows through my palm and into my chest. My breath catches. The llama exhales. I half expect it to speak. Something wise. Something cryptic. Maybe even something snarky.

But it just blinks, turns, and walks away. Dignified, like it's done its job. Was that a blessing? I tuck the memory into my pocket.

The trail curves gently, carved into the side of the mountain. Ferns brush my legs. The air smells of moss and rain. I raise my eyes and freeze.

The green stops.

The lush canopy gives way to something stark and wrong. The trees are brittle, stripped of leaves. The ground is cracked, gray, lifeless. It's not erosion. It's not drought. It's something else.

My heart stumbles. I step forward, kneel, and place my hand on the earth, just like in my dream. But this time, there's no pulse. No warmth. No memory.

The night before, joy had bloomed inside me. Bright and unexpected.

Now, it's gone.

The ground beneath my palm is cool and silent. The butterflies have vanished. Even the air feels heavier. I search for the feeling, the spark, the heartbeat, but there's only stillness.

It's like the joy was borrowed, and it's terrible.

Mateo approaches quietly.

One of the Canadians whispers, "Why is it like this? Why is the land dead?"

Mateo doesn't answer right away. He looks out over the hollow, his face unreadable. "The mountain does this. Every ten years or so. It starts dying."

"Why?" I ask.

He shrugs, reverent. "No one knows. Some say it's like a breath held too long. Others say it's hunger. Or grief. Like it needs something."

I press my hand on the ground, hoping for even a flicker of life. But there's nothing. Just stone cold and silence.

The bookkeeper's voice returns to me. Every step drains him.

My heart breaks. We did this. All of us. Our boots. Our noise. Our need to see and explore. I squeeze my eyes shut and try to hold back the ache in my throat. There has to be something I can do.

Then I remember...Huayna Picchu requires payment.

Hope blossoms in me. Maybe the payment is near, maybe it has already been made. I open my eyes and wipe my face with the heel of my hand.

A hand rests on my shoulder. Mateo's voice is quiet. "We should keep moving. We're losing light."

I nod. Not because I'm ready, but because I have to believe the mountain can survive.

Later that evening, I'm sitting by the fire. The fire crackles low, casting flickering shadows on the stone walls around our camp at Wiñay Wayna. The air smells of damp earth and woodsmoke. The stars above us are sharp and endless.

The ache from earlier still lingers. The silence of the mountain, the absence of warmth beneath my hand, left a hollow I can't quite name. I wonder if this land, so full of memory and spirit, will be here for future generations. Or will its voice fade, buried beneath footsteps?

But here, under the stars, something shifts.

The fire warms my skin. A breeze carries the scent of orchids. I feel the mountain again. Not loud. Not pulsing. But present. Quiet. Patient.

I close my eyes and hold onto that feeling. The mountain will survive. It has to. I open my eyes and breath in the night.

Tomorrow, we will reach Machu Picchu. My heart stirs with anticipation. We sit in a loose circle, wrapped in jackets and silence, waiting for Mateo to speak.

He stands slowly, brushing dust from his hands. His face is lit by firelight. It's creased, thoughtful, and somehow older tonight.

"Tomorrow," he begins, "we arrive at Machu Picchu."

A few people smile. One of the women claps softly.

But Mateo doesn't smile back. His voice is calm, almost solemn.

"We'll leave before sunrise," he says. "The trail to Inti Punku—the Sun Gate—is steep, but short. If we time it right, we'll arrive just as the light touches the stones."

He pauses, letting that image settle.

"And it will be quiet," he adds. "Empty. For a little while."

Someone asks, "How long before the trains arrive?"

Mateo glances at the horizon. "Maybe an hour. Sometimes less. The tourists from Cusco come in waves. But you'll have time. Time to walk the terraces. To sit with the silence. To feel what the ancestors felt."

I shift closer to the fire, heart thudding. I've seen photos of Machu Picchu, crowds, cameras, noise. But this...this sounds amazing.

Mateo looks at each of us, his gaze lingering on me just a moment longer.

"Don't rush," he says. "The mountain doesn't speak loudly. You have to listen."

No one responds. We just sit there, watching the flames dance, knowing tomorrow we'll step into something ancient.

Then, as the fire dims, Mateo adds, "The excursion ends at Machu Picchu. You're welcome to stay as long as you like. Your tickets will work for the bus ride down to Aguas Calientes. But if you feel something calling you...don't ignore it."

That night, my dreams are silent. But the mist grips my shoulders like a hug.

We reach the Sun Gate just as the sky begins to blush. I sit cross-legged on a worn stone ledge, cool against my skin, the moss damp from the night. All around me, the ruins are silent.

Slowly, the darkness softens. A pale blush spills over the peaks, brushing Huayna Picchu with gold. The mist curls like smoke around the mountains. I watch as the sun edges upward, shy at first, then bold, casting light across the stones.

The air shifts. The familiar smell of eucalyptus and wet earth reaches me. I close my eyes for a moment, letting the warmth touch my face. Birdsong breaks the silence. They are sharp, clear, like a call to wake. I open my eyes, and the ruins are alive now, glowing. The sun paints everything in amber: the grass, the stones, even the shadows seem to stretch with purpose.

I don't speak. I just breathe. And in this moment, I feel small and infinite all at once.

"I made it, Mom, and it's just as beautiful as you said it was," I whisper to the air.

I wander without a map, letting my feet decide. The ruins stretch out like a dream, terraces layered like green steps to the sky, stone walls that hum with memory. Every corner feels like a secret waiting to be found.

I duck beneath a low archway and enter a quiet chamber. The stone is cool here, shadowed, and I run my fingers along the grooves etched into the walls. I imagine the hands that carved them, the voices that once echoed here. It's like time folds in on itself, and I'm walking beside ghosts.

Outside, the light dazzles. I climb a narrow staircase and emerge onto a high terrace where the view steals my breath. The valley spills out below, lush and endless, and Huayna Picchu rises like a guardian. I laugh out loud, the young mountain, and he is beautiful.

Tourists begin to arrive, their voices floating through the air in a dozen languages. Some gasp. Some cry. Some just stand still, stunned. I watch a little boy chase a butterfly near the Temple of the Sun, his giggle ringing like a bell. A couple poses for a photo, their arms wrapped around each other, eyes shining. A woman kneels to touch the earth, whispering something I can't hear.

I wander away from the crowd and sit on a ledge and eat a granola bar, sipping water. I watch the clouds drift lazily across the peaks. A llama ambles by, utterly unimpressed by our presence. I remember my llama friend from yesterday, and I smile and snap a photo, but it's the feeling I want to remember. The peace and the joy.

I spend hours exploring. I climb to the Intihuatana stone and rest my hand on it, feeling the faint thrum beneath my palm. I walk the agricultural terraces and marvel at their precision. I find a quiet corner near the Sacred Plaza and lie back in the grass, letting the sun kiss my face.

Time stretches, and it is wonderful.

By late afternoon, the light turns golden. Shadows lengthen. The ruins glow. I hear music from a distance. I climb one last staircase and look out over it all. I turn, and there stands Huayna Picchu, its peak rising sharp and silent above the ruins. I'm going to hike it. The last thing on my list, and then I can leave.

I pass a small sign: *Entrada a Huayna Picchu.* My heart thuds.

The entrance is simple. A wooden arch, a rope barrier, a stone marker worn smooth by time. But it feels like a threshold. Like I'm standing at the edge of something ancient and intimate.

The ranger in a green vest studies my ticket and passport, then glances up at me. His eyes are kind, but knowing, like he's seen hundreds of pilgrims arrive here, each carrying their own silent question. He nods and lifts the rope. I step through.

Behind me, the world feels ordinary, with tourists chatting, cameras clicking, the hum of footsteps on stone. But ahead, the path narrows, climbing into mist and silence. It's as if the mountain has drawn a veil between realms.

The stone beneath my boots is ancient, worn smooth by centuries of ascent. The first steps are carved deep into the rock, deliberate and worn. I take a breath and begin to climb.

The path is steep, carved into the mountain's skin, and each step feels like a prayer. The higher I climb, the more the wind begins to speak.

"Clara…"

I pause. My name floats through the air, soft and clear, like it's been waiting for me.

"Clara…"

I take a sip from my water bottle, just in case it's altitude sickness. I keep climbing.

For all the bustle of Machu Picchu below, Huayna Picchu is quiet. Just a few casual climbers pass me, their voices hushed, their footsteps reverent. But mostly, it's me. And the mountain.

At the summit, the world opens.

Machu Picchu lies below, radiant. The river winds through the valley like silver thread. The sky stretches wide and endless. Wow.

My eyes keep scanning, and then I stop. Beyond the terraces, beyond the gold and green, there's a wound. A dark scar in the land. It's the death that I saw yesterday.

My heart breaks all over again.

A hummingbird appears and hovers before me, its wings a blur of emerald flame. I recognize it. My companion from the first day, it leans in and touches my cheek.

Butterflies rise from my right, golden and blue. I blink and smile. They spiral around me, just as they did near the waterfall.

A llama stands nearby, the same one that stared at me from the trail. Its eyes are deep and ancient. It doesn't move, but I feel its presence pressing into me.

Then the fox steps forward, red-furred and silent. It sits beside the terrace, tail curled, eyes bright with something like mourning.

The flowers bloom suddenly. Cantutas, lupines, and wild orchids burst from the cracks in the stone. Their petals stretch toward me.

I hear them; they are all reaching for me, and they are hurting, sad.

And then she appears.

The woman from my dreams is wrapped in woven cloth the color of twilight. Her hair is braided with silver thread, and her eyes are the same ones I've seen in sleep: kind, fierce, and full of knowing.

"You remember me," she says.

I nod. My throat tightens.

"You've walked the path. You've listened. That is why the mountain chose you."

Her voice is steady, ancient.

"The mountain is dying," she says. "Not in stone, but in spirit. Forgotten. Trampled. Its breath grows thin."

"I know," I say with a tremble in my voice. "But what can I do?"

She lifts her hand, and the terrace pulses beneath me. The hummingbird hovers closer. The butterflies spiral higher. The fox bows its head. The llama steps forward. The flowers tremble.

"Offer yourself," she says.

"What?" I ask.

"If you do not offer yourself, it will fade. But if you do..." She places her hand over my heart. It's warm. Steady. "You will not die. You will become."

I blink. "Become?"

"For ten years, your life force will serve as an anchor. A

tether between the sacred and the living. Every visitor who walks these paths will feel you—your joy, your reverence, your breath in the wind."

I swallow. "And after?"

"You will return. Just as you are now. No aging. No loss. You'll pick up where you left off, and the mountain will choose another."

I close my eyes. Ten years. Ten years without speaking, without being seen. No laughter. No school. I have no family to miss me, but I will miss the world. The taste of strawberries. The sound of music drifting in the air. The feeling of rain on my skin.

But then I see myself in the fog, in the hush between footsteps. I see children climbing Huayna Picchu, pausing to listen. I see a girl like me, years from now, placing her hand on a stone and feeling it thrum with memory.

I see myself there.

Not gone. Just changed.

I open my eyes and look out over Machu Picchu, glowing in the last light. Beyond it, I see the wound. The trees are dead and the land is grey.

A chill runs through me. I can't let this place be forgotten. I can't let it disappear, not when I can do something.

I smile at her and nod yes.

Moments later, Mateo walks into the clearing. He kneels down and picks up a red journal. He brushes off the dust, opens the worn cover, and reads the final entry. His eyes linger on the last line:

The mountain is not alone.

He smiles and whispers, "She said yes."

SIGNORA DE TRAGLIA'S FLESH AND BLOOD PIZZA
DAVID RODEBACK

The small sign she'd pounded into the lawn yesterday said, in an ornate but legible typeface, "Signora de Traglia's Flesh and Blood Pizza." She'd carefully placed it more than a foot in from the sidewalk in front of her old house to avoid the city's right-of-way.

It was bait, and it worked quickly. Now a slightly paunchy middle-aged man stood on her lawn, photographing her sign with his smartphone. His grey polo shirt sported a familiar blue-and-white city logo.

In previous cities, she'd tried to approach mayors and princes directly. But American cities didn't have princes, and too many small-city mayors avoided their people when they could. More often than not, lately, she entered through the back door. It didn't matter how she wiggled her way into a community, after all. It wouldn't limit her power.

She left the shade of her porch and approached the man. When she was closer, she could see that the embroidery under the logo spelled "Ghost Falls." The white pickup parked in front of her neighbor's home had the same logo, accompanied by block letters: "Code Enforcement."

"Young man, is there a problem?"

He examined her, but not in a leering way. She was only moderately wrinkled, for her age, but no one leered at her anymore. She saw that her blood-red shirt, with its intricate, not-quite-subtle, spiraling Old World pattern caught his eye.

"Are you Signora de Traglia?" He said it wrong, pronouncing all the *g*'s."

She pronounced it correctly. "The *g*'s are silent, more or less. The *g* in my surname actually changes the pronunciation of the *l*, but there's no equivalent sound in English."

She knew she sounded like a native English speaker, but for a slight lilt in her phrasing.

"I apologize," he said. "Are you aware that this neighborhood is not zoned for business?"

She nodded solemnly. "I have heard that the city is making exceptions, in deference to these difficult economic times. A most enlightened policy for a darkening time."

"We've never made an exception for a restaurant," he said. "Too much parking, and they generate too much traffic on the street."

"I wouldn't call my enterprise a restaurant."

He read from the sign. "Unique Pizza. Secret Old World recipes. By appointment, one party only, maximum six people. Seatings at 11:00, noon, and 1:00 p.m. sharp. Closed Sundays." He turned to her. "Sounds like a restaurant to me."

"It's not even a café, more of a tiny kitchen. I have off-street parking for two vehicles, and everything's up to health department standards. I have some experience with this elsewhere."

"Still, the traffic," he said.

"My neighbor sells Avon out of her home. She attracts about two dozen vehicles on an average weekday. I've counted. I have a maximum of six per day." She smiled graciously. "Would you care to inspect?"

"Very well."

"Follow me, please."

She led him up a gravel drive, along the side of the old brick house, into a different world—a few square yards of dense forest, or so it felt to her. A trellis was interlaced with vines, on which grew an unusual fruit in shades of brown, red, and orange.

"I don't recognize this fruit," he said.

Her mouth curved with a smile, but her eyes flared with something else. "It's not native."

He peered at a fruit from close range. "What is it?"

"In English, it's usually called blood fruit."

"Is it edible?"

"Oh, yes, even healthful. Rich in antioxidants, among other effects. It's difficult to grow here, but with a little magic, I manage."

"Blood fruit. Does this have anything to do with 'Flesh and Blood Pizza'?"

She produced the most restrained of her spooky smiles. "My secret recipe for the sauce—you must promise not to tell, but since you're a trusted public official I'll tell you— includes pureed blood fruit and the flesh of half a blood orange. I won't tell you the rest of the recipe."

She'd seen his uneasy look on others. Talk of blood and flesh in connection with food made some folks squeamish. She didn't mind. "Officer, who approves an exception?"

"Code Enforcement makes a recommendation to Zoning and Licensing, and the head of that department makes the final call."

"And who is the head of that department?" she asked, smiling beatifically.

"I am. Bill Stewart. Call me Bill."

She raised her eyebrows, and he added, "I try to get out into the city every week anyway, and our code enforcement officer is recovering from a knee replacement."

"I wish him well. But you seem like the sort of official I can work with. You said an exception is unlikely? I believe you said it was unprecedented."

"I should observe your business in operation. Have you applied for an exception?"

"The completed paperwork is inside. I have no reservation at 1:00 p.m. today, if you're free. You could bring up to five friends or colleagues. No more than two vehicles, please."

"We're not allowed to accept free stuff."

"I'll be happy to take your money, Bill."

"How much of my money?"

"It's *prix fixe*, ordinarily $16.66 per person, but $9.66 while I get started. You get a distinctive Italian side salad with my blood orange vinaigrette dressing, an 11-inch pizza with your choice of authentic toppings, and water or a soft drink. I don't have a liquor license. Today you may eat al fresco, on my lovely patio, or inside, in what I whimsically call the grotto. You will come, won't you, Bill?" She gently touched his arm.

He eyed her suspiciously. "I'll have to check my calendar."

She gave his arm a squeeze and let go. "Please do. Meanwhile, come inside."

Not for the first time, she relished feeling like the proverbial spider with the fly.

Two steps into the immaculate kitchen, he stopped. "Is that the sauce I smell?"

"It is. Do you find it pleasant?"

"Yes, absolutely. It's . . . I don't know the right word."

"Captivating? Entrancing? Seductive? Magical?" He never saw her fleeting smile.

He breathed deeply, then spoke slowly, as if dazed. "All those things. What's in it besides blood fruit?"

"I grow a certain tomato which has no equal in an American grocery store. Its juice has a particular tang, but equally important, its flesh gives the sauce a slightly different texture. I would very much like you to come for lunch at 1 p.m."

"I haven't been out to lunch in weeks. So okay, I will. Do you need to know how many?"

"Ordinarily, yes, but for the city I'll make an exception. Don't be late."

"I won't."

She picked up the city forms from the counter and handed them to him. "I don't suppose you could consider my exception before you come."

He nodded mechanically.

"And you'll approve it, won't you? You can always revoke

your approval later, if I try to turn this into an Olive Garden or a Texas Roadhouse. Or if you don't enjoy my cuisine."

Outside, he appeared to regain his strength. "Well, ma'am, there's still the precedent. And technically you should have filed it and received approval before you put up your sign."

"Oh, silly me. I should have realized. And I forgot to ask you something. Would you like to taste the sauce? It's nearly ready."

He nodded slowly and followed her back into the kitchen.

"Do you prefer to taste with a spoon or on a bit of bread?"

"A spoon is fine."

She pulled a spoon from a drawer, plunged it into the steaming pot on the stove, and brought it out dripping with the rich, blood-red sauce.

"Let's let it cool for a few seconds," she said. Finally, she offered him the spoon. He took it from her, inhaled deeply, then raised it to his mouth almost reverently. He took the whole spoonful at once.

He closed his eyes, drew in another breath, swallowed, and opened his eyes wider than before.

"Magnificent," he breathed. "So good it might actually be evil."

"Well said. I'm so happy you're pleased. You will formally approve my exception before you come."

He seemed dazed again. "Yes, of course."

"Excellent. I promise you a culinary experience you'll want to repeat. Perhaps you'll bring the mayor next time, and the chief of police and president of the school board."

"I'll be here promptly at 1:00. The sign can stay until then."

If a smile could be at once beatific and dark, hers was both. She'd practiced that for years in the ancient mirror her grandmother had passed to her. Others saw the beatific side; she reveled in feeling the dark side. "I'm so pleased. Thank you for dropping by. I'll walk you out."

She waved and smiled sweetly as he drove his truck away. Then her smile turned darker. "Another small step," she said to herself, and turned to go inside.

———

Bill was as good as his word. Just before 1:00 p.m., he appeared in the company of a sternly professional, forty-something woman and a man who looked decidedly blue collar and walked with a cane. The woman he introduced as Christina, his executive assistant. "She runs about half the city," he said, "but don't tell anyone." The man he presented as Jim, the enforcement officer. "He's off, but he dropped by, so I brought him for lunch."

"I am pleased to meet you both," she said. "Very pleased indeed."

She nodded subtly to herself. Things worked differently with women, but Christina would pose no great obstacle.

She seated them on the patio at a round wrought-iron table inlaid with black stone and handed them old-fashioned menus. She excused herself to tend to the sauce, while they deciphered the script and decided what to order.

In the kitchen, she opened a small packet and pulled out

a tiny disinfecting wipe of the sort sold to diabetics, rubbed it on the tip of the little finger of her left hand, and set it aside. She retrieved a tiny lancet and poked her fingertip. A small drop of blood appeared. She let it grow until it was ready to drip, then held it over a tiny stainless-steel cup.

Drip, squeeze, drip. Squeeze, drip, squeeze, drip. Four drops would do. There were thirteen in the sauce already, which would be enough for men but not a woman. She had wondered for ages about the difference. Was it physiological or spiritual? Perhaps both.

A few moments later, she appeared at the table to take their orders.

"What a lovely black crucifix you're wearing," Christina said to her, fingering her own silver crucifix on a silver chain.

"Christina goes to Mass every morning," said Jim. "Bill and I are heathens."

"I see," she said. She would add two or three more drops to the sauce for pious Christina's pizza.

"Is it metallic?" asked Christina. "Your crucifix."

"No, it's stone. Highly polished, of course."

"What kind of stone?"

"I suppose you would call it a gemstone, but I don't know its name in English. In Italian it means something like "Eye of Demon." It's fairly rare. This was handed down to me through the generations. Would you care to hear the old legend? Hardly anyone believes it anymore, and it's quite absurd, of course, but I'll be happy to tell it to you when I have your pizzas in the oven. What can I prepare for you?"

"We're having trouble deciding," Bill reported. "We thought we might go with what you recommend."

Her eyes flashed involuntarily, but they were all staring at their menus. She stared at each of them in turn. "The Diablo for you, ma'am. Just a hint of fire; there's a bit of something extra in the sauce." And a dash of something else to mask the iron taste of blood, she thought, in case Christina's palate was particularly discerning.

"For you, sir," she said to Jim, "the Purgatorio, a classic from my region of Italy. And for you, sir," she said to Bill, "the Vesuvio. No, on second thought, the Pompeii."

"All very exotic and historical," said Jim.

"Indeed, sir," she said. "There is nothing quite like them in the world."

She started them on their salads, then retreated to the kitchen. When the pizzas were in the oven, she returned.

"This is the most remarkable salad dressing I've ever tasted," Christina announced, with an enthusiasm she hadn't shown earlier. "I can hardly wait for the pizza."

"You have only about seven minutes to wait. Meanwhile, I'll tell you the legend."

She told them de Traglia was a pseudonym, adopted by the one woman in Pompeii said to have survived the eruption of Vesuvius. "The people from nearby towns," she said, "especially the priests, called her a witch. They blamed her for the eruption and the subsequent destruction. It was said that she opened a portal directly to hell, as revenge for some slight by the rulers of the city. They attempted to apprehend and burn her, but she reportedly escaped and was not seen there again."

She pressed her hand to the black crucifix. "The stone of which this is fashioned is found only in that region, usually near a certain set of sulfur springs. Another legend has it that some witches can use the black gemstone to control priests, bishops, princes, magistrates, and such—not so much against their will as controlling their will."

Jim chuckled. "Do you suppose they controlled any nuisance officers?"

"In my imagination," she said not quite candidly, "I think of judges who punish people harshly for committing crimes far less serious than they themselves commit without consequence, and rulers who care only for their own wealth and power, which they advance at great cost to their people." She felt herself growing too animated, so she stopped before mentioning the brutal public floggings, in town after town, of brave priests who railed against corrupt public officials, floggings even a priest's young siblings were required to observe. "I'm sure that could never happen here," she concluded.

"I would hope not," said Christina. "Civilization has advanced beyond all that. For example, we didn't blame magic for the Indian Ocean tsunami and the Haitian earthquake."

The woman's pedantic tone tempted Signora de Traglia to cite the Antioch earthquake of 526 A.D., which occurred on Ascension Day. They'd probably never heard of that—or far deadlier events. The Yangtze River floods of 1931, the Yellow River floods of 1887, the Jiajing Great Earthquake of 1556, even the Bhola Cyclone of 1970.

Instead, she rewarded their rapt attention with an appropriately wicked smile. "Of course, the modern world knows all that is ridiculous, but that's the legend and my name's origin too. I'll fetch your pizzas."

Half an hour later, she took their payments—three separate checks, predictably. None of them needed a box; her patrons hardly ever did. By then, their enthusiasm for her creations was quite ardent, but more of a quiet, obsessive passion than a source of bubbly exultations. She felt her eyes flash darkly again but supposed they didn't notice.

"You will come again, no later than the week after next," she urged, "and bring with you the mayor and the chief of police. Bring the president of the school board too, if you can."

"Of course," said Bill. "Bet my life on it."

"Indeed," she mused. "When they're here, I have matters to discuss with them about the future of this charming city, and some things they might wish to do for me in coming weeks."

All three guests nodded obediently.

"Thank you for coming," she said as they reached the city pickup in the driveway. She offered each a firm handshake, which she knew belied her advanced age. "Before I clean up and cast the refuse into the fire—so to speak—I shall invoke an ancient blessing on your day."

As she watched the truck pull away, her little finger throbbed deliciously, and the spark in her eyes turned to fire. She softly chanted a few of the ancient words. She would chant the rest, and more loudly, when the time was ripe.

MEMORIES OF SORRENTO
ANDREA TILLMANNS

"Mom," said Marie, "the poor flowers are completely dry."

Her mother looked up from the ironing board. "The flowers on the balcony? I know, sweetheart."

She would water them later, after she had put away the ironed laundry. One thing at a time, otherwise she wouldn't be able to get through the day's work. The part-time job as a secretary, which she had taken on again after Marie started school, took up a lot of Anna's time and energy.

Marie shook her head vigorously. "No, the flowers in Grandma's picture."

It took Anna a moment to understand what her daughter meant. In the hallway hung a picture with dried flowers and insects from a long-ago vacation in Italy. At the time, Anna herself had been a child and had enthusiastically pressed the colorful flowers and grasses in books to give the picture to her mother someday. She couldn't remember exactly where the insects had come from. Presumably, the butterfly had not survived the winter and had been found on a windowsill or in a dark corner at some point, just like the two gnats and the ladybug. Perhaps they came from Sorrento, just like the flowers on which they were glued.

"Those are dried flowers," Anna explained, turning her attention back to the blouse under the iron. "They have to be this dry." She ignored Marie's doubtful expression.

———

"The flowers are doing much better now," Marie remarked cheerfully the next day at dinner.

It was only later, when she looked closely at the picture with the dried flowers, that Anna understood what her daughter had meant. The flowers seemed to have regained some of their original color, and the green leaves no longer looked quite so flat and stiff. Anna carefully touched the brown cardboard strip she had glued to the bottom of the picture to imitate the ground. It was damp and left a slight brown tinge on her finger. Nevertheless, the wallpaper behind the picture looked undamaged. If Marie had actually watered these flowers, she had been very careful.

It was only a few days later that Anna happened to see her daughter filling a toy syringe with water and going into the hallway with it. Later that evening, when Marie was already in bed asleep, Anna checked the picture and the wallpaper behind it.

The brown cardboard strip was now much rougher and more uneven than before; it actually looked almost like soil. Most of the plants had now detached themselves from the crayon-green background and seemed to be leaning their heads toward the window opposite. If Anna hadn't known better, the flowers would have seemed almost alive to her.

———

"The butterfly is moving!" Marie announced excitedly one morning. "Do you think it will manage to free itself?"

"If it wants to, it will surely manage it," Anna assured her. It wasn't a lie; she simply didn't believe that a butterfly that had been dead for years would want to free itself from the picture.

The next morning, the butterfly was gone.

"It flew away, it actually did it!" Marie exclaimed as she rushed into the kitchen and hurriedly sat down at the breakfast table.

"The butterfly probably only speaks Italian and can't find its way around here at all," her mother pointed out. She wanted to discourage Marie from removing the other animals from the picture as well.

When she opened the window in the hallway the next day, it didn't take long for another butterfly to flutter in and settle on one of the flowers in the picture. It had obviously succumbed to the same optical illusion as Anna, who found the plants appearing more and more lifelike. Sometimes, when she looked at the picture out of the corner of her eye, she thought she saw the ladybug slowly moving a leg or the long wings of the gnats trembling in the wind.

The next time she opened the hallway window wide, all three insects disappeared at once. Marie complained briefly that she had gone to play with a friend that afternoon of all days. The ladybug returned the very next day, and with it came a few bees, buzzing quietly as they flitted from one flower to the next.

Anna wasn't very surprised when she noticed the small black and brown seeds below the picture. She carefully scattered them all in the flower box she had placed there in the hallway.

When the sun was shining, they left the window in the hallway open so that butterflies and other insects could fly to their picture. Sometimes Anna wondered what her neighbors or colleagues would say if they could see the picture, which was overgrown with grass and flowers and smelled like summer all year round. But when she sat on the hallway stairs in the morning before waking Marie and watched the insects slowly awaken in the first light of day, she didn't care much.

6

LUCKY PENNY

E.B. WHEELER

"You brought a metal detector to a cemetery?"

My brother Mark looked up from the trunk of his car with a grin. "This whole place is crawling with history."

"It's tacky," I said. "Is it even legal?"

Mark only shrugged and pulled out the metal detector.

A chill brushed over my skin despite the August heat, and I rubbed my arms. Rows of tombstones stood in front of me like weary petitioners waiting their turn at court, all faded, many tilting. Yellowed cheat grass and scraggly bindweed were all that managed to dig roots into the hardpan soil between the markers.

Mark came up behind me, metal detector resting on his shoulder.

"Look at this, Jenn." He pointed to the markers. "See how many are from June 1902? One of the mine shafts collapsed. Dozens of men and boys suffocated. It wasn't the worst disaster in the West, or even in the state, so people have forgotten it now. Like this place."

I couldn't help smiling. "But not your students, right?"

"Right! I think they understand history better when I show them it's about real people."

I crouched by three graves. The shadow from my hat cut the glare so I could read the names. All Davies. Welsh. A father and two sons, based on their ages.

I stood and stretched my back. Which was worse: to lose your husband suddenly to an accident or slowly as he fell out of love with you and into the arms of another woman? I thought Mrs. Davies probably got the better deal. At least her pain was long behind her.

I turned away from the markers. "This place is depressing."

"Grief leaves its mark on places, and 1902 was a bad year for them, but they had their community. That's what helps people through these kinds of disasters."

I squinted at the desolate landscape. A jackrabbit darted behind a distant sagebrush. "There's no community here now."

"Well, that's what you want, right? A quiet place to start over? There are some cheap parcels of land for sale around here. Recreation lots for people who want to four-wheel or have a base camp during hunting season. Totally off grid."

That *was* what I wanted. There'd be nobody here to judge me—or let me down. I grimaced at the thin layer of dust coating my sneakers. Did being alone have to mean living in such an ugly place?

Mark had moved away from the cemetery and was

waving his metal detector over the old road. Its occasional beep was the only thing breaking the near-perfect hush of the arid landscape, the quiet strange to my ears. He stopped to pick up something from the bushes, examined it with a squint, then tossed it aside and resumed his searching.

I wandered closer to watch.

"What do you hope to find?" I asked.

"Anything interesting left behind. A button, a buckle. Things like that. I ask my students to imagine the people who used them—what their lives were like."

I nodded absently. Mark's house was jammed with "interesting" things he'd found out in the desert. Pieces of old bikes, broken watches, tin cans. Most of it seemed like junk to me, but Mark collected and displayed it like he was the Smithsonian. He even had a cabinet of green uranium glass. Thank goodness he never asked me to eat off it.

After a few minutes of wandering, sweat rolled between my shoulder blades. I had serious doubts that this was the right place for my tiny home. I was installing solar panels, so being off-grid was ideal. But I was going to have to haul water in unless I could dig a well, and I doubted that was in the cards out here. I didn't want to rely on water trucks.

"Any luck?" I asked.

"Nothing much." He looked around in resignation. "It's like the desert scoured this place clean. Or it's been picked over already."

I shrugged, ready to go.

He shaded his eyes with his hand. "You wanna give it a try?"

"Not really. You know about the petrified wood curse, right?"

"Jenn, you can't find petrified wood with a metal detector."

"That's not my point. I mean, if it's bad luck to take petrified wood from national parks, how much worse would it be to steal from a graveyard?"

"We're not in the cemetery. And this area is BLM land, so recreational metal detecting is allowed, as long as we're not taking Native American artifacts or anything like that." He held out the metal detector. "You want to leave, right? Give it a shot, and if you don't find anything, we can go."

I sighed and grabbed the metal detector. "Fine."

I swung the gizmo back and forth over the ground like I was sweeping the kitchen.

"Slow down!" Mark instructed. "You're not going to find anything that way."

I smirked. That was the point. But to play fair, I slowed my sweep. I stepped out of the roadway but stayed well away from the cemetery. I was not a graverobber. I'd leave that to the archaeologists.

The metal detector let out a high-pitched whine, and I almost dropped it.

"You found something!" Mark bounded to my side. "That could have been gold. Find it again."

This was silly. I wasn't going to find a treasure in the desert. But as I swung the metal detector slowly over the ground, the whine picked up again. I held the position. I'd found something. My heartbeat picked up, and I shared an adrenaline-fuelled grin with Mark. No wonder he was addicted to this.

Mark made an X on the spot and took the metal detector, handing me a little spade he carried like a dagger at his belt. I knelt in the dirt and hammered against the hard-packed earth.

"It won't be down very deep," Mark said over my shoulder.

"Good," I grunted.

But I realized I would have dug if I had to. I wanted to know what I'd found.

After a few mini shovelfuls, Mark said, "There!" He picked a dirt-encrusted object from the tailings. "It's a coin."

"Gold?" I asked, laughing at myself.

He brushed the coin off. "Sadly, no. A nice Indian head penny, though. It's worth a couple of bucks."

I held out my hand, and he dropped the penny into it. It was cool compared to the heat of the day. I brushed off more of the dirt, revealing the date. 1902. I glanced back at the cemetery. Had some mourner dropped it here during the funeral? Or when they came to visit their family's grave? For a moment, I imagined a column of wagons carrying coffins up the road, mourners trudging behind.

"I'm not sure I should keep it."

"You have to. It's a lucky penny. You know, 'Find a penny, pick it up, then all day, you'll have good luck.'"

I rolled my eyes and shoved the penny in my pocket. "Fine. We can still leave now, right?"

"Yeah. At least the day wasn't a total waste."

———

I waved to Mark after he dropped me off, then sighed and turned to my current residence. Not my "home." After being out in the open space of the desert, my little townhouse apartment looked even more cramped. The tiny house on its wheels, taking up my cracked and weedy driveway, wasn't much smaller. Luckily, after the divorce, I had very little left. I'd had a bonfire for everything that reminded me of Jake.

The elderly lady in the townhouse next to mine was the only person around. She was weeding the little flowerbed that constituted a yard in this neighborhood. She was the only one who bothered.

"Hello," she said as I walked past.

I nodded in response. I wasn't going to be around long enough to bother chatting or making friends.

This is the third time he's gone off the wagon. The drugs are going to kill him.

"What?" I asked sharply.

"I said hello," the woman said, looking almost as confused as I felt.

"I'm sorry... I just thought..." I shook my head. "I guess I was lost in thought. Have a good evening."

"You too."

I don't know what to do for him. Am I a terrible mother?

I gave a start and looked back, but the woman had her head bent over the weeds, her shoulders stooped. Maybe she was whispering to herself, but it was more like the words had blossomed in my mind. Prickles raced up my arms.

I had to wiggle my key to make it fit in the old lock. I

slammed the door behind me and shut all the bolts, tossing my keys on the table.

I took a long breath. I was probably dehydrated from being out in the desert. I filled a glass at the sink and chugged it down.

My fridge was mostly empty, though. I needed to run to the store. That was one way it would be tricky to be self-sufficient. I needed land where I could have some chickens and a garden.

For now, though, the grocery store down the block.

I hurried out the front door and almost slammed into the grumpy guy a few doors down.

"Watch it," he grumbled, keeping his shoulders hunched and his head down.

What's the point of any of it? Why bother going on?

Had he muttered that? Or was I hearing things? Was I spending too much time alone? Letting my imagination run wild? I could *not* have a mental breakdown. Jake would smirk and say he always knew I was crazy. No, I was probably just exhausted.

I tried to keep my visit to the store quick. It's not like anyone there was likely to know that I was the woman who couldn't keep her husband, but I didn't want to take any chances. I grabbed a few staples and hurried for the line. This little place didn't have self-checkout, so I had to deal with a line and a cashier. I stood behind a guy who seemed kind of out of it. Bloodshot eyes, not very steady on his feet as he loaded his groceries onto the belt. Lots of junk food, like he had the munchies. I tried to stay out of his way, but the lady behind me was crowding forward like she could make us all go faster, and the guy bumped me with his elbow.

"Sorry," he mumbled.

Another week or two, if we're lucky. Dammit. Screw cancer. Screw it, screw it, screw it.

I blinked and shook my head. He definitely hadn't been speaking aloud. His mouth was pinched into a thin line.

"Hey, Billy," the cashier said. "How's your dad?"

"He doesn't have much longer," Billy muttered.

"I'm sorry to hear that. He's a good guy."

Billy nodded and pulled out his wallet.

It had to be a coincidence, right? Those thoughts about cancer, and this guy's dad only had a week or two?

Billy hugged his bags to his chest and shambled out of the store, and it was my turn.

The cashier started ringing me up. I hesitated, then broke one of my rules. I engaged in conversation.

"It's sad about his dad," I said casually, trying to act like I knew Billy and his father.

"Oh, I know!" the cashier said, pausing in her scanning to shake her head. "Cancer's a bitch, huh?"

I nodded, but goosebumps raced over my skin. Cancer. Maybe it was a coincidence. Maybe my brain was trying to understand why the guy looked like he was having a rough time. And cancer wasn't so uncommon...

Who was I kidding? I'd thought the guy was strung out on drugs.

How had I known about the cancer? Was I developing some kind of telepathic empathy from being alone too much? Or just losing my mind?

I mumbled a thanks when the cashier handed me my receipt and hurried home with my groceries. Once again, I locked the door behind me. This time, those little bolts didn't look very substantial. I shoved the groceries in the fridge and then paced.

I wasn't going crazy. Crazy people didn't wonder if they were crazy. They also didn't know what people were thinking about. And I didn't think hallucinations came on so suddenly. This had just started this evening, since I got back from Mark's excursion. I folded my arms as I paced, then shoved my hands in my pockets. My fingers brushed the penny.

An odd sensation came over me. I thought I heard weeping, and my chest ached at the sorrow, but at the same time, it felt like hands held me up.

I pulled the penny out and stared at it. The sense of sorrow—and of support—slowly dissipated. I stared at the coin. The Indian head on the image and even the reeding around the edge of the coin were crisp and sharp, safely buried well over one hundred years ago, though the copper had turned dark from its long burial. I rubbed my finger over the ridged edge, and the sound of weeping once again filled my ears.

The penny *was* cursed!

"I knew it," I mumbled.

Just tell me what I did wrong!

I gasped. Those were the words I had screamed at Jake when all of my suspicions were confirmed. My own words echoed around my head. It was like the coin was playing them back, some kind of macabre recorder of sorrow.

Definitely cursed.

I almost threw it across the room, but I couldn't quite bring myself to do it. Because, despite how it made me feel ill to have any reminders of Jake, the coin radiated warmth. Comfort.

So, was it cursed? It seemed to reflect back sorrow. Grief. I should just set it aside. I had enough of my own to deal with without needing to hear everyone else's. Cancer. Drugs.

But what about my neighbor, Mr. Grumpy? He'd almost sounded suicidal. I didn't want to get involved in anyone else's drama, but I couldn't ignore that. I also couldn't just walk up to Mr. Grumpy and ask if he was depressed. Maybe the penny would show me more of what he was thinking?

I held the penny and pictured the guy, but nothing happened. Did I have to be looking at him in person for it to work? I thought back to my other encounters. Each time I'd heard someone's thoughts, I'd been close to them. How was I supposed to get close enough to Grumpy to hear what he was thinking?

I stepped outside and looked around, hoping I'd be lucky enough to run into him. But of course, it couldn't be that easy.

My gardening neighbor was back to work, though. I hesitated. I didn't want any connections in this temporary stop. Maybe if I could get her interested in Mr. Grumpy's problem, she'd take him off my hands.

As an experiment, I walked closer to her and listened. Nothing.

"Hello?" I said.

She looked up. "Good evening."

I don't want him to die.

The weight of her sorrow and worry slammed into me. No, I couldn't do this. I already hurt too much. I hadn't heard anything until she spoke to me. So, I would just avoid speaking to everyone.

Ugh. But after I'd set up some help for Mr. Grumpy.

"Hi," I started, shifting uncertainly. "I wondered if you knew anything about the man who lives in that apartment." I pointed.

She concentrated on the apartment. To my relief, no more of her grief flowed into me. Maybe she was distracted from it now.

"I see him around sometimes, but I don't really know him. Why?"

"I... overheard him muttering something. He sounded like he's not doing okay. I'm not sure... I don't know if I should call the cops for... what do they call them? A welfare check? I don't want to cause problems. I don't know for sure that he's struggling."

She sighed and set down her weed fork. "I imagine he is. Isn't everyone struggling these days?"

"So, you think I should ask for one of those checks?" That would get him help, right?

She sighed and dusted off her shorts. "I don't know. People can only change if they want to. And sometimes even then, it's not enough."

"Then... there's nothing I can do?"

She stood. "I didn't say that. Have you tried talking to him?"

"Well, no. He doesn't seem very friendly. And I don't want him to think anything about my intentions, you know?"

"Oh, yes, I see. Well, I'm an old lady. He won't think I'm trying to flirt with him."

I sighed to myself and smiled a little. She was going to help him.

She linked an arm through mine. "Let's go to my place and make some cookies."

"What?" I almost jerked my arm away.

"Almost no one will say no to cookies. Unless he's got one of those intolerances. I've got a recipe that uses oats instead of flour. More of a cookie bar, but it's gooey and delicious."

"You think he just needs a treat?"

"No, I think he needs an excuse to talk to someone. Come on."

I'd started this, so I didn't think I could get out of finishing it. It was just some cookies, and then we'd cure Mr. Grumpy, apparently, and I could put the penny away and go back to minding my own business.

"I'm Alice, by the way," the gardener said.

"Jennifer," I responded automatically. "Or Jenn. Not Jenny."

Jake had called me Jenny. I was done with that name.

"Okay, Jenn."

She guided me into her little apartment, a mirror of mine, though she had vases of wildflowers on her table and pictures on the wall with what looked to be a husband and a son. A folded and framed flag displayed next to a picture of the husband in a military uniform told me he had been gone a while. The son must be the one she was worried about.

She handed me a bowl and a whisk and gave me instructions as we assembled the cookie bars. They looked delicious, and smelled even better when she slid them into the oven.

"I've seen you working on that little trailer house," she said while we waited for them to cook.

"Oh, yeah. That's my long-term plan. You know, go live somewhere less...crowded."

"It would be nice to have a real garden." She sighed and glanced at the pictures on the wall. "I've thought about moving out to the country somewhere. It's harder when you have kids, though."

I nodded. No connections. That was the way to live. Though, I couldn't help comparing the bareness of my walls to the colorful displays on hers.

"Your husband was military?" I asked, nodding to the flag.

"Yes. I miss him. At least I still have my son." Her eyes clouded over for a moment, then she shook off whatever dark thought had seized her. "He's an artist. Very talented. It's a hard way to make a living, though. Easy to get distracted."

I nodded. "I studied art in school, but I went into marketing. My ex—" I shook my head. I didn't want to talk about Jake and how he ridiculed everything that wasn't practical. "Well, some people don't appreciate creativity."

"It's best to keep those people out of our lives, isn't it?"

We sat in silence—but not uncomfortable silence—for a few minutes until the oven beeped.

"We'll have to let them cool before we can put them on a

plate, but here..." She scooped up a bit of the hot, gooey, delicious-looking mess and offered it to me.

I took the spoon and blew on it until I didn't fear for my mouth, then sampled it. I almost melted to the floor over how good it tasted. How long had it been since I'd had anything this delicious? I never cooked anymore, and when Mark invited me over for dinner, it was usually BBQ something-or-other.

"That's amazing," I said between licks of the spoon. "Mr. Grumpy will definitely talk to us for these."

Alice laughed. "You call him Mr. Grumpy?"

My face warmed, and I turned away to rinse off the spoon in the sink. "Well, I didn't know his name."

"Who was I? Old White Hair?"

I chuckled. "The Gardener."

"Oh, that's not so bad."

I wondered what people thought of me. The cold woman who's always alone? Pathetic Loser?

Alice plated the cookie bars. "It's time."

"You think he's home?"

"He's always home in the evenings. One thing being The Gardener does is give me time to notice people."

I nodded, realizing how lonely Alice must be, noticing everyone but speaking to no one.

We walked over to Mr. Grumpy's apartment. Alice was holding the cookies, so I had to knock. But I quickly stepped back to let her do the talking.

At first, I thought he would ignore us. I could hear the TV, but there was no sign anyone was moving inside. I had a terrible flash of worry that we were too late. But then the door slowly swung open.

"Yeah?" he asked suspiciously. He did not look well.

I can't handle one more thing.

Alice put on a chipper smile. "We wanted to get to know our neighbors better, so we brought you some cookies. Cookie bars. There's no wheat or nuts, in case you're allergic."

He just stared at us for a long time, like he was trying to decide if we were for real. Then his attention fixed on the plate. "Uh. Thanks? I'm not allergic."

"I'm Alice, and this is Jennifer." She pressed the plate into his hands.

"Uh, Steve." He stared at the plate and then at us. "Well, thanks."

He swung the door shut. At least I didn't hear any more dire thoughts from him.

Alice and I walked away.

"That seemed like a promising start," Alice said.

I nodded. But it would be a promising ending for me as well. I had done something for Steve Grumpy, and for Alice, and now I could be done.

———

That Saturday, I went to work with renewed energy on my tiny home. I needed to get out, get away from people. Alice waved to me from her garden, and I waved back. But I didn't talk to her. I didn't want to hear any more sad thoughts. I was curious if she'd seen Steve and if he was doing better, but I wasn't going to be drawn in. No attachments.

I had enough to worry about with my tiny home. I was trying to get the solar panels hooked up, and it was well outside of my comfort zone. I pulled up some DIY videos on my phone, trying to make sense of all the connections and the information about voltage.

I glanced up at one point to see Steve watching from his window. I probably looked like an idiot. After an hour of struggling, I was ready to throw the stupid, wobbly solar panels into the street for the joy of watching them get crushed by the traffic.

I groaned and rested my head on my arms, then looked up again. Steve had come out of his house. He stood there awkwardly, holding Alice's empty plate. I almost snapped at him, asked what he was staring at, but he walked past me to Alice to return the plate.

"Those were good. Thank you."

"Of course! I'm glad you liked them, and we're glad you're here in our little neighborhood."

He shrugged, looking skeptical, and started back for his place.

He paused when he passed me again.

"Hey," he said. "I don't want to be one of those people, but do you want some help with that? I've done some electrical work."

What a joke. I'm such a useless piece of crap. That's why they laid me off. Why Stacey left me.

I swallowed my initial impulse to say no. I did need help, and maybe he needed to be helpful.

"Sure." I stepped away from the tiny house. "Yeah, that would be great. I'm over my head here."

He looked surprised for a moment, then stepped up to take my place, quickly going to work to sort out the mess I'd made.

Alice came up beside me. "Good idea. Everyone needs to feel useful."

I almost laughed. Did she think I'd been bad at this on purpose?

But Steve did look happier as he went to work on the panels. He had them installed pretty quickly.

"Thanks!" I said, and I meant it.

"Sure. That's pretty easy stuff."

I laughed. "Not for me." But his sorrowful thoughts had stopped. An idea struck me. "I have some more electrical work to do. Could I pay you to help me? I know you're probably busy..."

"Not that busy. Sure, I'll do it."

I thought about the tiny house forum that I lurked in, not wanting to post and make any friends in the community. I'd joined the community to get away from community.

Before I could stop myself, I said, "I might know of some other people who need help as well. Other tiny home people. If you want me to pass on your number."

"Uh, sure."

He texted me his number, and luckily didn't seem to take it as flirtation. I would just pass his information on in the forum. No need to do more than make a quick post about a guy who was good with solar panels.

———

A couple of Saturdays later, Alice brought us cookies full of gluten and melty chocolate chips while Steve showed me how to make sure my heater was working correctly.

"Thanks for passing on my number," he said. "I've been looking for a job, and it's been good... One guy even said he might have more permanent employment for me."

"That's wonderful!" Alice said, taking one of her cookies.

If only I could help Matthew.

I gave her a keen look. I'd heard fewer sorrowful thoughts from Steve, but I wished I could help her as well.

"How's your son?" I asked tentatively. "Working on any projects lately?"

She sighed. "I'm afraid not. He...he has some struggles with addiction. He's trying to get clean, and when he does, he can create, but then his old friends come around..."

Steve nodded. "I've seen that with my brother. He had to move to a new city to get a fresh start. Make different friends."

"I've wondered about that," Alice said. "But artists don't make much money, so he ends up crashing with the same guys. If I had a bigger apartment, he could stay with me. But it would be so cramped, I'm afraid he'd move back with his old friends pretty quickly. He needs at least a little of his own space."

We sat quietly. I shoved my hands in my pockets, and my fingers brushed the penny. The feeling washing over me again, the weight of sorrow eased by support, the sting of pain lessened by empathy and friendship. I could almost see those miners' families crying together, holding each other. Helping each other. Community.

Then, almost without my permission, my mouth said, "He can stay in the tiny house."

"What?" Alice asked.

What? I asked myself. I looked up at the tiny house. It was my ticket to freedom. But...it wasn't finished. And, I wasn't in as much of a hurry as I had been to leave. I was keeping busy, and I hardly ever thought about Jake. When I did, it didn't seem to hurt as much. I couldn't gauge my own thoughts and grief like I could with Alice and Steve, but I had a feeling I'd be hearing less of my own sorrow, too.

I took a deep breath. "He can help me test it out. Stay here, let me know if he runs into any problems. Once he's back on his feet, he'll be able to afford his own place, and he won't have to go back to the guys who get him in trouble."

Alice's eyes filled with tears. "That would be wonderful! And he could make new friends here. This is a wonderful little community."

A month ago, I would have rolled my eyes at that idea. But it was a decent little place. He might hit it off with Steve, and if not, there were other people in the area he could connect with. It might be the perfect place for someone to heal. After all, it had a good support network.

THE FATE OF BEAUMONT TURNER
KAREN DENT

No one knows what happened to Beaumont Turner, but the legends say he pays his penance down in the Hollow.

———

June stood at her stove and stirred the warming milk, hoping she had enough chocolate to make cocoa. She glanced over at her son, Jediah-Clemment, sitting in the corner of the kitchen, staring at nothing she could see. T'were'nt new to her. He was seeing with his gift.

Her heart ached, and she stirred the milk vigorously, thinking, *Jed's a good boy. Quiet, thoughtful, and at six years two months, too darn serious for his own good.*

His straight, black hair hung over his forehead, hiding his eyes, and she knew she'd have to cut it before Beaumont came home from his hunting trip.

Beau'll more'n likely be hungry and nasty, full of himself and his manly abilities. Jed's hair would be the perfect beginning to start something.

She sighed, took the scalding milk off the burner, and set it aside. She reached into the cabinet and brought out the cocoa tin and pried off the top. *Good. Enough for three and leftovers in case Beau wanted some when he got home.*

As she spooned out the cocoa, she watched her son get up and walk over to the playpen where little May was gumming her teething urges on the bars. He picked her up and kissed her while she showed her appreciation by yanking his hair.

Yep, I'm definitely cutting that today.

She didn't blame her husband for his hatred of his son. It was just his daddy genes told him Jed wasn't his. It weren't something she ever admitted, and it weren't something he found out about. He just knew, and year after year, he tried to get her to admit it.

"I understand you was lonely, June bug. Really, I do. I was gone a coupla months," he'd say, looking all expectant. Then, at her silence, he'd get god-fearing angry, *"Fess up now! The Lord tells us we have to confess our sins in order to be redeemed!"*

But nothing, not even the beatings or violent alcoholic rages, would get her to tell. So, he had to live with a suspicion that poisoned him in a slow steady stream till he ended up like he was now—a bitter and ugly man.

The sweet smell of cocoa filled the kitchen, and she poured it into two mugs, plus a small baby bottle, and checked its heat. May stuck out her chubby hand, squeezing her fingers open and closed for the unexpected goodie.

MayBelle hadn't made a sound since she was born, didn't

even scream when Ellie smacked her bottom and sponged off the birthing goop from her eyes.

June thought back on the forty-eight-hour labor only to hear silence at the end.

———

She lay in her bed quietly sobbing, believing she'd given birth to yet another dead child. She hid her face, and while her tears ran freely, she prayed.

"Thank you, God, for Jed. Thank you for sending me at least one —"

But Ellie didn't let her finish.

"Hush now, June. Look. Look at how beautiful she is. She's perfect. A perfect angel after all your woes." And she laid little May beside her. "She don't say much, but that's a good thing. Won't get no sass when she grows up," she laughed.

June held her and said, "She's deaf then?"

"Don't' think so. Snapped in both ears. She heard. Just think she's gonna be a quiet one. An' she's got good tolerance for pain. For a woman, that's always an extra gift."

———

"Mom?"

June started out of her memory when Jed held up his cup. She smiled, and they clicked.

"Cheers," they said together, a secret tradition they'd started when he was three.

Jed held the baby on his lap as she drank happily, kicking

her feet rhythmically, snuggled into the slight recess of his thin chest.

Their love for each other was a joy to behold. June's eyes misted over, and she looked away. She was going to break that bond. And it had to be soon.

June had decided to send Jed to her sister to live. Beau was drinking too much when he was home and increasingly violent. After he'd hauled off and smacked Jed unconscious, she'd calmly gone to the shed, come out with his hand axe, and while he was sprawled out on his comfy chair, smashed it down between his legs.

He flipped over and scrambled against the wall. "What the Hell?!"

Her voice shook with her own repressed rage as she said, "No more Beau. You touch either one of us again, and I'll cut them off and let you bleed to death."

His lips broke into a sneer, then twisted to something more fearful when she added, "If you hurt us again, you better kill me, 'cause if you don't, you'll wake up without 'em. And we both know you won't be nothing without your boys."

June knew this threat would ring true because of what happened to Samuel down in the Hollow. Folks still talked about that, and it happened over 50 years ago. No telling what a woman stretched to her last nerve would do to a man.

June shook off the memory and took the cups to the sink. "Jed, grab my scissors and cutting towel. I can't see your beautiful eyes with all that hair hanging in 'em. And don't forget to pick up your stuff. Your dad'll be home soon."

Jed dutifully did what he was told as she washed up.

She was going to miss him. She felt peaceful with him around. She'd prayed for a miracle and was truly answered.

She remembered the day like it was yesterday.

———

Walking the six miles home from the small church, her knees ached from kneeling and desperately pleading for a healthy baby, promising anything in return.

Her thoughts turned to the ramblings of Grandma Margaret. "Don' ever ferget, Junie, witchy women is in our blood. Church is good for men folk, but if you pray to the land with your heart and soul—you'll be hurd."

'Heathen talk," her ma scolded.

But now, June closed her eyes and prayed. "Forgive me for whatever I've done to deserve my sorrows. Please hear me," she whispered.

When she opened her eyes, there stood a man, someone who wasn't from around these parts. They stared at each other for a while. Then he smiled, and the sunlight hit his ragged coal-black hair and lit his turquoise eyes to shining stars.

When he gestured for her to follow, she knew her prayers were answered.

Silent, they walked and burrowed deep into the cool woods. She let him undress her and watched as he stripped. She thought he looked like a man made of braided, palm leaves, muscles twisted and roped beneath thin skin.

His touch was gentle, like he'd never seen nor touched a woman's body before. He laid her down in a soft bed of moss, softer than any bed she'd ever been in, and she knew right then, they were going to make a healthy baby.

The sun dappled through the thick leaves, turning his naked body green. His muscles rippled oddly, and she breathed in the cool scent of the forest, and forever more would think of him when the damp, dank smell of good earth traveled down from the Pines.

When it was over, she closed her eyes and said a prayer of gratitude, knowing this would bring her a strong, wholesome child. Then said a prayer for the four babies that died at birth.

She tried to remember their faces as she said her prayers, the one with no arms and twisted spine, and the other three whose heads were misshapen, and wondered what else the Land would ask of her in return. Surely, all her babies buried back into the earth was enough.

She drifted into a light sleep, never hearing the Straw Man leave, rocked as she was by the soft crooning of the leaves above.

———

June shook herself out of the past. *Wish I could tell the future,* she thought as she soaped the pot with the scum of milk clinging to the edges.

Her mother didn't need the sight to know Beau had bad blood.

"All I'm sayin' is his family is queer with sickness."

That had started the fight. Fool that she was, she'd run out of the house with her mother yelling, *"His mama had sixteen children, and only four survived past age one. Do you want that misery, June Marie? His family's tainted!"*

But Beau was beautiful. And funny, charming, dangerous,

and sexy. There was no way she believed her Beau could be anything but perfect. Except now, two of his sisters had some blood disease that caused the shakes, and the third one looked like she might be coming down with it too. She should have listened to her ma, dead now these past three years.

Beau came slamming into the house just as June swept up Jed's hair. She walked past him, sniffin' the air as she passed to see how much he'd been drinking. He reeked of whisky, and his bloodshot eyes watched her. Both of them stayed silent. As far as she was concerned, silent was always good, but could turn bad later.

She hadn't told Jed about living with his aunt, but when she walked into his room, he was sitting on his bed, his meager belongings neatly packed in a cardboard box. She went over and hugged him hard, kissing his head. She allowed herself one fleeting wish it could be different, but knew she needed to do this for him as well as for her.

"Don't you worry none 'bout May."

Jed twitched.

"Now don't fret. He loves her an' won't do nothing to hurt her." She stopped, realizing what she'd said. "An, I'll be goin' back to make sure." She took a deep breath. "Let's go then," she whispered.

They started toward the front door, but Beau stepped in their way with his shotgun. "Where the hell you think you're goin'?"

"Don't start, Beau. Jed's going to visit my sister for a while, that's all."

"So, I come home and you leave? Bull shit!" He grabbed

Jed and yanked him from June's hands, flinging him across the floor. "You're staying right here. Or," his eyes slit down to cunning, "are you planning on sneakin' off with his daddy again?"

June looked at him and realized her mistake in waiting this long. He'd had enough to drink to make him stupid and reckless. *There'll be no reasoning with his crazy-ass self holding a shotgun* she thought. She looked past him at Jed who stared back with a silent understanding. June shrugged and turned to Beau.

"Fine. I made cocoa before, you want some?" She walked to the stove. "I'll cook up whatever you brought back, but it'll be a while." From the corner of her eye, she saw Jed retreat to his room.

Beau swayed on his feet, and she watched surprise cross his sweaty face at her easy capitulation. He plopped down at the table and parked his gun across his lap.

"Coffee and Jack," he demanded, slamming his fist down on the table for emphasis.

June put the flame under the aluminum pot and took the bottle of Jack Daniels from the cabinet. She put it and a mug in front of him. "What'd you bring back?"

"Squirrel," he muttered, annoyed with himself. "Not much else out there these days." He glared, defying her to add her usual smart-mouthed remark.

This time, she just thought it. She heard the soft slip of a window being raised and knew Jed would be waiting for her out back.

"Fine. I got some potatoes and greens we can have with it." She walked back to the stove and grabbed the shrunken potatoes with shaking fingers. If Beau suspected they planned to defy him, they might actually end up dead.

She shoved the potatoes into the oven and got out the greens while he poured his mug half-full of liquor. *Go ahead,* she thought, *make it easy.*

She rinsed the greens and put them in a pot. "I'll get the squirrel."

She wiped her hands on her apron and left. He eyeballed her but stayed seated, sipping the whisky.

As soon as the door slammed behind her, she ran around the back, grabbed Jed's hand, and they took off. Even drunk, her husband was a good tracker, especially when he got all fired up for a chase.

They crashed into the woods and flat-out ran. It would be three miles before they reached her sister, and she didn't know how long it would be before he hound-dogged after them.

Her sister's husband shook his head when she told him her plan, "Don't ask me ta pick either of you up. Beau's your husband and he's got rights." At the look her sister gave him, he added, "But if you get here on your own, he won't be takin' you back without your say so."

June'd smiled at him and was mighty glad at least her sister married a good man.

She and Jed ran for twenty minutes with no sound following. Her son kept up surprisingly well, and she allowed them to slow to a jog. They stopped when she got a powerful stitch in her side and had to bend over to knead it out. Her lungs burned enough to make her feel like throwing up.

"Better keep moving," Jed said, "he's comin' and he's mad".

She heard nothing but didn't question how Jed knew. They sprinted and looped through a tangle of saplings, weeds, and gnarly tree roots in a secret path June had made in the deep woods that cut off a quarter of a mile from their journey. She hoped Beau wouldn't notice, and she'd taken pains to leave false clues further along the straight path these last two weeks just in case. Her grams' warnings still came to her when she slept, and she never had no reason to ignore them.

They crashed through a shallow stream, startling a deer that bounded off through the thicket toward where they had come. She cursed and hoped it would be decoy instead of their downfall.

They heard rustling and softly muttered curses. The loud explosion of a gun vibrated the forest around them. The scream of the dying deer carried in the still night.

Jed stopped and looked back, his big eyes full of unshed tears.

She ran back, grabbed him, and whispered, "That fine Buck gave its life for you, Jed. Don't make it regret it."

They dashed away while Beau's heavy-footed crashes retreated the way he'd come.

Winded and sweaty, they came to the clearing before her sister's house. June could see the lights twinkling, looking like they'd lit every single one they had. It shined like hope, and June felt the pain of love swell in her chest.

Jed uneasily scanned the patch of tufted grasses and waving brush. They stepped out, set to cross the sea of waving grasses. The thunder of a shotgun shattered the night and exploded a tree stump next to June.

Slivers of bark and dead wood flew out and stabbed June's bare legs and arms. She froze.

Beau stepped out across the way, moonlight winking off the barrel of his gun. His eyes glittered as he strode closer. June and Jed twisted to run back the way they'd come. He fired again. This time at the tree beside Jed.

"Stay!" he commanded June, "or your son'll be lying dead at your feet."

June pushed Jed behind her. The trees that circled them began to sway. A howling wind picked up and bent their bows with a summer storm's ferocity. But the air held no smell of rain. No thunder or lightning cut through the sky. Only the angry wind made a fuss.

Beau reloaded, then slowly walked toward them. He pointed his gun. "You're gonna tell me tonight, Junie, who fathered your bastard child or, so help me –"

She shook her head in denial.

"If'in you don't – you're both dead. I'll tell 'em all you run off with some fancy pants man and bury your sorry asses so no one'll find you."

She knew he'd do it. He had a wild, hard set to his jaw she'd never seen before.

Silently, she begged, *please Straw Man, save our son. I don't mean nothin' in this world, you can take my blood an' flesh, but let our son live.*

Jed peeked out from around his mother. He stared behind Beau with surprise.

Uneasy, Beau shifted his feet but didn't turn.

"What the hell you looking at boy? I'm right here and this," he hefted the gun higher, "is the only thing you ought to be starin' at."

June also noticed something happening behind Beau. A twirling of wind and twigs circled to the right of him. A small whirling tornado edged toward them. It took on the vague shape of a man.

Stubborn, Beau stayed facing them while the wind clawed at his hair and clothes. He watched June and Jed fight the gusts that yanked at them, too. Leaves and dead grasses flew into his face with determined speed. He shielded his eyes and ignored the low moan behind him. It built to a shrieking roar before Beau spun around just as the moving Dust-Devil touched him.

Beau shot it and screamed obscenities while parts of him disappeared into the roiling mass.

Buckshot splattered June, and she sank to her knees, a last smile for her son upon her face as her blood soaked the dry earth and disappeared.

———

No one knows what happened to Beaumont Turner, but the legends say he was swallowed up by the Straw Man and pays his penance by haunting the Hollow with Samuel. For how long, no one knows, but Jed goes there on occasion. He tells folks it's to help Beau along his path.

When the wind stirs up, there is a fearful moan that echoes through that Hollow.

A human sound, not unlike Beau Turner.

EL COYOTE

TJ TARBET

"And after they had tasted of the fruit they were ashamed, because of those that were scoffing at them; and they fell away into forbidden paths and were lost."

- 1 Nephi 8:28

He tried to read on, but the next verses in the *Book of Mormon* seemed to slide off his mind. *Fell away into forbidden paths and were lost.*

That verse had always felt different to him. It didn't say that they'd left God's path to join the Great and Spacious Building, which was an allegory for the World. No, instead, they went some other way. It called to him. Forbidden paths, esoteric knowledge. Some third way that was neither transcendence nor damnation, just cold solitude and the exploration of things beyond God's purview.

Laughter came from the next room where his mission

companion and district leader were playing poker with the stolen rent money. And probably some of his. He wasn't sure, though. He seemed to be missing some, but the thought of counting his stipend made him squirm like an insect laid bare after his rock was moved.

Judge not, lest ye be judged.

This wasn't where he'd expected to be halfway through his calling as a Mormon missionary. He'd expected his mission to be hard, but not like this. Everyone talked about how challenging the mission field was, but most of it had been about hunger, long days, rejection, and heartbreak as he and his companion worked diligently to bring souls unto Christ. Setting an example, studying scripture, calling people to repent. They were supposed to be devoting themselves entirely to Christ, with no thought to their life, or what they would eat, or even their clothes, just like Jesus commanded his disciples in Matthew.

Instead, he felt like he was being dragged along by the Prodigal Son. His companion, Elder Mendoza, hadn't spoken to him except in grunts and eyerolls since he'd gotten here. Instead of paying the rent, he'd kept it for himself, and when the landlord kicked them out, they'd had to move into their District Leader's apartment. Every time he suggested they go out and actually try to talk to people, find new investigators, or even just do service projects, his companion had looked at him like he was a particularly stupid child that he'd been stuck with.

The Lord hadn't been much better. He'd prayed, begged, pleaded for something he could do. What was he doing wrong? What could he fix? But God seemed as silent as his companion, and as contemptuous.

His mind came back to the verse. *Fell away into forbidden paths and were lost.*

He didn't feel lost. He felt empty. Gone. Erased. Like he never was. The memories of his family were a distant echo, and his weekly letters to them were a ritual of putting on a brave face. He felt like he could just walk off into the desert and be gone. They might miss his emails, the same way one might miss a small-time radio personality, but then he would be gone, like a whisper in the desert.

A coyote yowled in the distance, and a shiver ran down his spine. He pulled the blanket closer around his shoulders. The heaters were in the other room, where the other Elders gambled away the rent and their stipends in laughter. He was always cold now. They hadn't bought natural gas to fuel the water heater since before he'd arrived, and they didn't even have one of those little electric heaters with which to heat the little washing buckets. But he couldn't judge. He was just the arrogant gringo, come down from the North. Technically, he wasn't even supposed to be alone, and the excuse of separating himself from the gambling and the music seemed as empty and hollow as his own soul.

Another roar of laughter came from the other room, and behind it the coyote called again. He'd never heard a coyote call in his time in Mexico, much less in the middle of the city of Queretaro. But now he could hear it, even through the thick cinder block walls.

He was tired. He was always tired, no matter how much

he slept. Sleep was his only escape from the nightmare he was in, one where his own companions hated him no matter what he tried, where he couldn't even go off and do the Work of bringing souls unto Christ on his own. What was he to do? He couldn't even tell anyone. That was the first rule of the mission. One of two. *Thou shalt not tattle.* Like most real rules, it had never been told to him, only observed. Not that it would help, anyway. Sure, he could go to the Mission President, but what would he change? His companion was a *frito,* a missionary who'd given up, who didn't care. Who was whiling away the last few days until he was sent home. Even if he said something, the Mission President only had so many tools. He could either call them both in and give Elder Mendoza a stern talking to, which meant that Mendoza would turn and take it out on him, or send Mendoza home early in disgrace.

He didn't want to be the reason why a missionary was sent home early. He'd already been that once before, when his first companion had been caught having sex with a girl, and he'd been called in as a witness. He didn't want that again.

Sleep was his only escape. So sleep he did. He curled up in the blankets that were too short for him and closed his eyes, listening to the calls of the coyote and the laughter of his companions.

———

He awoke shivering. He'd slept late; the other Elders were already up and about, despite their late night. Despite this, he lay in his little cocoon for a while longer, tempted to just roll over and descend back into the dreamless sleep and be lost. Lost. That verse came back to him again. *Fell into forbidden paths and were lost.* That didn't sound so bad, honestly. He'd tasted of the Tree, supposedly, but all he felt was hollow. And he certainly didn't receive any divine guidance on what he was supposed to do, or how he was supposed to call his companions to repentance. Even that felt arrogant. Who was *he* to call them? He was sleeping late, spending time alone when he was clearly supposed to be trying to help them. They were supposed to be calling souls to Christ, but they seemed determined to do anything but.

He did get up eventually, though, shivering in the dark, his breath dewing in the morning air. That did surprise him. Of all the things he'd thought about Mexico, *cold* certainly wasn't one of them.

He dressed in the same clothes that he'd worn the day before. And the day before that. Threadbare dress pants and a button-up shirt. The only trace of himself was the choice of tie, which choked him more and more every day. But he wore it anyway. What else was he to do?

The other Elders pointedly ignored him when he came out of the room. The room he was supposed to be sharing with his companion, the companion who wouldn't even look at him, much less speak to him.

Like most houses in Mexico, the place they were renting was a *casa con patio,* and it was cold. It was a series of rooms arranged in a square, with a central patio that was open to the sky, and full of trash; at one point, it might have just been a stopgap for Elders that hadn't had the time to bring the trash out for collection one week, but now it was nearly knee high and full of stench. A single sapling rose from the plastic *bolsas* of rotting things, more like a twig than a tree. He was surprised it was alive at all; it might not have been. He'd never been willing to wade through the trash to check. At the edge of the patio sat a bucket of frozen water. His companions were laughing and joking as they tied their own ties, talking about music they weren't supposed to be listening to and girls they weren't supposed to be looking at.

He tried to break the silence.

"Did you guys hear the coyote last night?"

His District Leader, Elder Morales, scoffed. "Que? No hay coyotes aqui." *There are no coyotes here.*

He blushed and pursed his lips, looking down. Of course they hadn't heard; stupid question. Even if he hadn't imagined it, they would have been too loud to hear it. He shrugged. "I thought I heard one," he said lamely.

Elder Morales just rolled his eyes. "Nececitas dormir con nosotros," he said seriously. *You need to sleep in the same room as us.* He pulled his tie into a knot, somehow managing to look down his nose at him, despite being nearly a foot shorter. "Es contra las reglas a dormir solo." *It's against the rules to sleep alone.*

And gambling with the rent money isn't against the rules? he thought. But he held his tongue. Held his thoughts. Who was he to judge? Technically, Elder Morales was right. It was against the rules to sleep alone. He shrugged. "Okay."

Elder Morales turned away, and the other two followed him, himself last of all.

———

They piled into what Mexico called a bus, or rather a *combi* - a little van, stripped to the bones and lined with as many seats as possible. He didn't ask where they were going. It didn't really matter at this point; he didn't have a choice in the matter. As he was just about to pay the driver, a sticker on the dashboard caught his eye. A coyote, surrounded by stars, with three white eyes, staring at him. A chill ran down his spine, and he blinked. When he opened his eyes, he couldn't find the sticker again.

The ride was brief. Instead of going out to find people to teach, they went into the center of town. They were going *shopping*. He didn't know where his companions were getting all this money. The missionary stipend was just a thousand pesos a month. But even so, Elder Morales and his companion went off to the Electronics section. When he came back, he had one of the latest cameras.

"Where did he get the money?"

Mendoza shrugged. "Con la renta," he said. *With the rent.*

He heard the *yip, yip, yip* of a coyote off in the distance, echoing like a laugh.

Con la renta. His mind reeled. So that's how Mendoza had convinced Morales to let them stay at their apartment. He'd bribed him with this month's rent money.

Elder Morales was bent over a baptismal form, filling it out. The tricolor carbon copy paper was folded and rumpled, and he paused on occasion, as if thinking. He hadn't seen them go out and do any teaching; they were together nearly all of the time.

"You guys had a baptism?" he said.

"No," Elder Morales said, not looking up.

He stared at Morales for a long moment, his mind churning, desperately trying to reach for a legitimate explanation.

"Are you... filling it out for the Bishop?"

"No."

"Was it someone who'd been baptized, but wasn't recorded?"

"No. No existe." *He doesn't exist.*

He felt hollow. Empty. As if his skin were a mere covering, stretched over bones that hid a cold and aching void. He didn't even know what to do with that information. He just stared at his district leader as the man filled out the form as if it was the most normal thing in the world. He heard the coyote call again, and this time it seemed to echo inside the empty reaches inside him, like he were nothing more than just the cold, empty desert.

He fell back against his seat, looking out the window once more. As the bus slowed to round a corner, he spotted something. A coyote with milky eyes sat on a pillar. It must have been blind, or so he thought. But still it met his eyes and watched as the bus rounded the corner, and he watched back.

————

Several days later, Mendoza elbowed him awake as they were riding on the bus. He hadn't been sleeping well, worrying about the rent, the falsified baptismal forms, and he was even more tired than usual. And when he did sleep, at least at night, the coyote with the milky eyes hunted his dreams. But in his dreams, the coyote's eyes were not milky. They were lunar, shining with an inner light that was somehow both reflective of, but different than the moon that always rose behind it. It watched him, a dark silhouette before the moon, before the stars, standing on an infinite glassy plane that seemed to ripple like water.

He shook his head and rubbed the sleep from his eyes, then hopped up. Mendoza hadn't waited for him. He was already at the front of the bus. An actual bus this time, not a stuffed, rattling *combi*. He jogged to catch up, quickly paying the bus driver another 25 pesos that he couldn't afford, then climbing off.

Mendoza walked on, his hands in his pockets, the messenger bag he carried on his shoulder empty. His was full; he didn't know why he kept it full. They never tracted, never handed out Books of Mormon, and the single solitary family that they "taught" already had a copy of *Another Testament of Christ*. But since they were *supposed* to be preaching, he carried them anyway. As if the mere presence of the books might coalesce some opportunity, some small chance to do good, some small seed he could plant. He hiked his heavy bag higher on his shoulder and jogged to catch up.

He walked behind Mendoza like a duckling, not beside him. Mendoza had taught him that lesson three days in. When he'd tried to walk side by side with his companion, Mendoza either sped up or slowed down, silently refusing to walk *a lado* with the *gringo*. So now he trailed behind him like a pack mule, carrying the burden that he had laid upon himself.

It was the rainy season in Queretaro, and it was cloudy and cold. The neighborhood they walked through was sparse, at the top of a large, steep hill that overlooked the rest of the valley, and full of naked dust. Queretaro was a lot like his home, Utah, in a way. Dry, dusty, mountainous. He clamped down on any twinge of nostalgia or homesickness he felt, for he knew that would destroy him. But still, the only time he felt at ease anymore was when he took a moment to look out over the valley and just... breathe.

The gravel roads were mostly even, but the houses were not. Bare cinderblock and rebar, rarely more than a single story, with cavernous holes where the doors or windows would be, covered by a string and a blanket.

They entered one such home, surrounded by a rickety fence, following the lady of the house. There was a dog with a metal chain for a collar, chained to what passed for a doghouse. The dog, a Doberman, charged them. Charged *him.* He jumped away, and it stopped at the end of the chain, straining and snapping silently as it glared at him.

I've tasted you, the dog seemed to say. He rubbed his inner thigh where the dog had indeed left his mark while Mendoza ducked inside, above the whole thing. A dead coyote lay in the corner of the yard, the dust-stained black and the dry yellow teeth glinting in the open air.

He followed.

The interior was not much better. The living room was small, with two adjacent rooms, a dirt floor, a sofa and some soft chairs that felt out of place, and a cot in the corner.

He didn't know why they were here again. Mendoza's pride, he guessed. "Voy a bautizarles," he'd told the family once. *I'm going to baptize you.* Which was strange to him, for his "lessons" never included any scripture at all, biblical or otherwise. And the Virgin Maria looked down at them from her little shrine in the corner.

It was a family of three - a husband and wife, and his brother, who'd been hit by a car and now had a leg that would no longer articulate. He tried to justify it every chance he could, pointing out how stiff and painful it was, and how he could not work because of it. He talked about it so frequently and earnestly that it seemed even to him that he was not being honest about the extent of the injury.

But the man did walk with a limp on the rare occasion he would get up from the cot. So he didn't press him on it. What was it to him if this man was lying to his family, anyway? They all seemed content with the situation, and he wasn't there to stir up trouble. *Judge not, lest ye be judged.*

Mendoza and the family talked about... things. Everything. Nothing. Whatever it was, it had nothing to do with Christ or even religion in general, beyond the most banal observation that all faiths point in the same direction. He couldn't pay attention. He'd tried to help teaching them once, bringing up a verse or two. Mendoza had glared at him like an idiot, then continued on as if he'd said nothing at all.

Their conversation slid off his brain like a monsoon off the asphalt, but at least he was warm. It felt like these "lessons" were the only time he was warm anymore, and he quickly slid off to sleep.

The coyote was there. Some part of him recognized that it was the first time the coyote had invaded his daytime dreams, which were usually brief and dreamless. It stared at him with those eyes that glowed white, the moon framed between its ears as if perched there. It said nothing. It did nothing. He wasn't even sure if it was breathing. It felt as though he was not, paralyzed as he felt himself being lost in those white, glowing eyes.

You are failing. The words echoed in his mind. He tried to breathe, to sob, to fall to his knees and beg. *What am I supposed to do? What words am I supposed to say? How can I get him to see?*

How do I get him to not hate me?

The coyote chuffed but did not blink, did not move. It just stared at him, like it could see all the flaws in his soul. The weakness. The uselessness. Like he was himself built upon a foundation of straw.

You were never meant for godhood anyway.

He woke with a start. The brother laughed. "Gringo dormión." *Sleepy gringo.* He said nothing, but the heat rose on his face. The brother laughed again. "Ni nos entiende, verdad?" *He doesn't even understand us, right?*

He did understand them, but he said nothing still. What would he say? Retort like a child? *Si, les entiendo.* Better to say nothing at all. It was the end of the "lesson" anyway. His companion just rolled his eyes and continued on, but the brother interrupted.

"Quiero darles algo," he said. *I want to give you something.*

He squirmed in his chair, uncomfortable. They weren't supposed to accept gifts from people. *Therefore take no thought, saying, What shall we eat? or, What shall we drink? or, Wherewithal shall we be clothed?* The verse echoed in his mind, and he felt a strange tension in his mind between it and the mission rules.

"Ustedes nos dieron un libro. Entonces quiero darles esto." *You gave us a book. So I want to give you this.*

He pulled out a book. It was surprisingly nice. A hardcover, deep green embossed with gold filigree. The title read, *El Primer Libro de Enoc.* The First Book of Enoch.

They definitely weren't supposed to take *that.* He recognized it. It was apocrypha. Not necessarily wrong, but...

The brother grinned. "Ustedes siempre estan hablando de mas verdad, mas conocimiento." *You're always talking about more truth, more knowledge.* He hefted the book, his eyes never leaving Mendoza's face. "Pues, aqui hay mas, no?" *Well, here's more, right?*

His mind stumbled at that. Was he really wrong? He'd heard of the apocryphal books before. Supposedly, they had truth, or at least some measure of it. Less than the canonical books, perhaps, which is why they weren't included in the King James Bible, but still... And the brother seemed to be giving it genuinely; this wasn't like a JW, trying to get them to accept their own mistranslated and mutilated version of the Bible. He simply took what they said as truth: more truth, more knowledge is always better, isn't it? Mendoza smiled and took it before he could think of something to say. But he didn't open it. He just thanked him and got up. It was time to go.

They shook hands all around. Even the brother rose from his cot, stiff leg held out before him like a rod, just long enough to shake their hands, then sat back down again. But the whole time, he felt his eyes being drawn again and again to that book. It seemed to burn in his companion's hand, and his curiosity itched like a healing bone in the back of his mind. What *was* in there?

A whispered verse came to his mind. *"Fell down forbidden paths and were lost."*

Mendoza scheduled their next appointment. Neither of them jotted it down; this family was their only investigators, and he didn't really have much of a choice in where they went anyway.

Then Mendoza left, and he followed. Thunder rumbled as they left the little hovel, and he wondered if it would rain again. Mendoza was off, walking down the gravel road at twice his usual pace. When they were halfway to the bus stop, he tossed the book into a trash can without a second glance.

He stopped, stunned. The book might not have been *scripture,* but it was still a *book.* It didn't deserve to be treated like that. He came from a family where they had more books than shelves, and someone was always reading something. But he had never seen Mendoza read anything that wasn't a map. And to see it tossed aside with such callousness was like watching someone strike a child. He stared at Mendoza's back as he walked on, blinking. Then he looked at the book. He couldn't just leave it there. It merited more respect than that. He licked his lips, then snatched it from the trash and stuffed it into his bag like contraband. Mendoza never looked back.

He jogged to catch up with his companion, the gravel crunching and the thunder rolling overhead. He'd never heard thunder in Mexico, but now it seemed like it wasn't going to stop. The street they walked down was

Huitzilopochtli, the ancient Aztec god of thunder, and at the moment, the name seemed appropriate.

They got to the bus stop and waited. Cars sped down the thoroughfare, the largest road that he'd seen in Mexico. But across the street, watching them, was a coyote. Mendoza seemed to not see it, or not to care, but he couldn't keep his eyes off it. As they waited for the bus to arrive, the thunder rumbled closer and closer, though no rain fell, and all the while the coyote watched. He couldn't tell if it was the same coyote as before, for it was too far away to see if it had milky eyes or not.

The bus eclipsed it as it arrived, and by the time that he ascended the steps, the coyote was gone. The bus hissed and the brakes squeaked as they disengaged, and in that sound, he thought he could hear the yowling of the coyote.

———

When they got back to the house, he laid the book right next to his English scriptures on the plastic shelves that passed for his dresser, his nightstand, and his desk all in one. Mendoza didn't even notice. He was already laughing with Morales and his companion in the other room.

He knew he would be expected in that room. He couldn't be alone, after all. It was against the rules. But the book called to him. It had been so long since he read something, anything that wasn't scripture. He'd finished the *Bible*, *Book of Mormon*, and *Doctrine & Covenants* several times over by this point, and his mind itched for something new, anything new.

It would be fine, right? Sure, it wasn't technically scripture, but it was close enough. A shallow excuse, but his mind was so parched for something to read that it seemed good enough. He sat down on his bed and cracked it open.

It was in Spanish, of course, but that was no real impediment. Contrary to what his companion thought, he *was* fluent in Spanish, and he did all of his scriptural study in it, had done so since three months into his mission.

When he opened it, he found that it was laid out much like the *Bible* or *Book of Mormon* was. Dual columns, verses, and even cross references with biblical texts at the bottom. It fell open to the eighth chapter, and before he could rifle back to the first page, his eyes fell on a verse.

3 Amezarak taught all those who cast spells and cut roots, Armaros the release of spells, and Baraqiel astrologers, and Kokabiel portents, and Tamiel taught astrology, and Asradel taught the path of the Moon.

The Coyote. He saw it in his mind's eye, a silhouette against the moon, those eyes shining with that same pale light. A shudder ran through him, and that verse came into his brain again. *Wandered down forbidden paths and were lost.* But the voice was small, and far away, and, most importantly, his own. It wasn't the still, small voice promised in the scriptures. No, it was his own voice, the one that he heard whenever he might do something against the rules.

But then, something else, something *other* resonated deep in his hollow core like a bell, and the words that the Coyote had spoken to him in his dream came again.

You were never meant for godhood anyway.

He stared at that verse for a long time, unseeing. Or,

EL COYOTE   113

rather, his mind was elsewhere. Drawn to that crystal plane and the star-sprant sky and the coyote staring at him.

When his companion barged into the room, he didn't know how long he'd been sitting there like that, enraptured away into his own little waking dream.

"Vamos a los tianguis," he said. *We're going to the market.* The first words he'd spoken to him in weeks, and said with a callous contempt that chilled him. Like he wasn't even worth speaking to, like an announcement spoken over an intercom. He didn't mention the book, didn't seem to care.

He snapped the book closed and checked his watch. It was late, almost 9:00 PM. Well past dark, and well past the hours where missionaries were supposed to be about. But they were going, and he had no say in it.

He patted his pocket; he was low on money. He still had some on his shelves, but when he checked how much he had, he swore it was less than before. He frowned. The numbers seemed to slide off his mind like everything else did nowadays. He counted again. No, there was definitely less. He glanced into the hallway where the other three stood, laughing and joking. It was his fault for leaving it out, anyway. *Judge not, lest ye be judged.* He pursed his lips and tucked the remainder of his cash into his pocket and joined them.

They walked out without ties, without nametags, and he followed. It was a short walk, and the full moon was up. When they got there, the open-air market was already crowded, bustling, packed with Mexicans who came no higher than his shoulder. He felt like Gulliver among the

Lilliputians, unwanted, unneeded, and every step he took felt like he was going to crush someone or destroy something.

None of the stalls had anything that interested him, but his companions filed among them like children. He didn't follow. He could see them just fine over the sea of black haired heads, which was more than enough for both him and them, apparently. Just enough to not be "alone."

His mind wandered as they shopped, drawn back to that verse from the Book of Enoch. *Asradel taught the path of the moon.* The path of the moon. What did that mean? What was such a thing? He knew Asradel was supposed to be an angel, or at least that's what he inferred. He didn't recognize most of the names listed in the verse, but he knew that Tamiel was an angel in some traditions, so the rest of them must be too.

Asradel...

"Prestame dinero." *Lend me money.* He jumped, breaking free of his reverie and looking down. His companion was looking up at him. "Quiero comprar algo." *I want to buy something.*

He fumbled at his wallet, feeling nothing. His companion's voice held no venom for once, but he couldn't bring himself to care. The money hardly seemed real anymore. Nothing did. He pulled out a 200 peso bill and handed it to Mendoza, who took it without thanking him. It was only $20 USD. Much more valuable to Mendoza than it was to him. And if this was the first step towards mending their relationship, then it was worth it.

A while later, they all went back to the house together. But instead of thanking him, Mendoza had gone back to ignoring him completely, and the other two didn't seem to care, or even know. Not that it even mattered. You were supposed to do good deeds because they were good, not for recognition. And yet, he felt hollow inside. Useless. Worthless. He looked off into the dark as they walked back. The full moon was still up, and the sky was full of stars. He thought he heard something following them in the distance.

He wondered what it would be like to just... go. He could stop right now, let his companions walk back to the house without him, and they wouldn't even notice. And he could just wander. Alone. Free. No pressure, no weight, no sin. Just... alone. He heard the yapping of the Coyote off in the distance, but if his companions heard it, they gave no sign. He paused for a moment, watching, listening. But it did not come again. The night was still. Cool. Empty. It seemed to match the state of his own soul. It was cold enough that he should be shivering, but he wasn't. He could just go. No one would stop him. No one would miss him. And by the time his companions were forced to reveal the truth, that they'd simply lost track of him, he would be gone. Even if they did lie about what had really happened, it wouldn't matter to him. He wouldn't be around to hear it. He'd be gone. Lost in the night. Somewhere else. It almost didn't matter, as long as it was away from here.

But no. He couldn't do that. He'd always been the "good" one. The one who followed the rules. He shook himself and looked up the street at his companions, then jogged to catch up.

———

"Pinche gringo," Mendoza said as he threw a wad of *billetes* at his chest. He caught what he could, but some of them puffed and fluttered like a wad of feathers, floating down to the ground. Pesos were a colorful currency, and they drifted down like a garish autumn of pinks and blues and greens. He stood there, aghast, but his companion was already gone, disappearing into the bedroom where the other two waited for him, already doling out the cards for their next game of poker.

He stood there, swaying like an empty bell. He felt... disconnected. Divorced from self and sound and sight. Nothing moved in that little patio, nothing but himself and the sapling and the plastic bolsas of trash fluttering in the cold night air.

His limbs moved, though he did not direct them. His knees knelt and his hands pawed the ground like a blind man, gathering up the fallen bills like leaves, and stacking them mindlessly. His fingers and arms moved on their own, and his eyes saw nothing as his hollow fingers moved among the stones of the patio, searching for the oddly sized bills that he did not feel. The waxy plastic felt strange in his hands, and he only picked them up because the ground was not the place for billetes to be.

He felt lost. Gone. Abandoned in every way that mattered. He uttered a desperate, wordless prayer in the back of his mind, hoping for something, anything from on high. *Help me. Please. Just give me something.* But no still small voice came. No comfort. No peace. Only the words of a hymn from his childhood, half remembered and echoing from a place far away in his soul.

I am like a star shining brightly...

But even that echoed away in the hollowness, and his hands fell limply to his sides, the billetes spilling out of his hands once more. The stone was cold under his knees, and the air was thin with a chill that seemed to mirror the emptiness inside him.

He didn't know how long he knelt there under the open sky, next to the bags of trash. Even the smell of the garbage did not seem to reach him through the cold air. All was still and cold and empty, and the only sound was the muffled laughter that came from the other side of the door.

That and the sound of the coyote laughing.

He rocked from side to side. What more could he have done? He was supposed to be a missionary. Bringing souls unto Christ. But he wasn't even strong enough for this; a companion who didn't even hate him, just ignored him.

And after they had tasted of the fruit they were ashamed, because of those that were scoffing at them; and they fell away into forbidden paths and were lost.

Was he ashamed? Or simply unworthy? He didn't know, but even the Holy Spirit didn't deign to notice him. He felt no promised comfort or peace. No direction. No still small voice. It was like his own soul was as empty as the desert itself.

A brief thought crystallized in his mind, then.

He needed God, made covenants with Him, chosen His way as best he could, despite all his faults and foibles. But now, when he needed Him most, there was nothing. Not a whisper. Not even a spark. Just a desperate attempt by his own mind to cling to the whispers of the past like a child clings to his blanket.

That meant one of two things. Either God did not exist, or He did not care about him.

Either way, the result was the same.

The coyote yowled again, closer now, and for the first time in a long time, he felt something calling to him. Forbidden paths. Not of sin, nor some celestial promise. Something different. Something other.

Well... He'd not broken his part of the covenants he'd made with the Lord. He'd striven and sacrificed and repented. He'd gone forth and baptized in His name. And yet, there was nothing.

He felt something watching him in the dark. Something calling to him. He would not be one to kick against the pricks, but neither would he strive to climb a mountain when he came crashing down to the base of it again and again.

He rose, leaving the billetes where they fell. His tie joined them, and his shoes and his nametag, then he stepped out into the cobbled street. The night was chill and moonless, but he did not shiver, and no mist rose from his breath. The bare stone was cold and hard and slippery beneath his feet. But with each step, he felt something of himself shedding, dropping away. Nothing replaced it, and each step he took, he felt more cold and hollow than before until he felt as though he was little more than starlight falling on the empty desert.

He walked. For hours or days or years, he couldn't tell, climbing, climbing, climbing that old hill that is Queretaro. And when he finally reached the top, the moon rose and the desert stretched out before him, cold and empty.

The Coyote was there, waiting for him. It stared at him

with cold, lunar eyes, three where there should be two. They watched each other for a while as the moon rose above the eastern peaks, and the whole valley lay awash in the pale light. Then the Coyote's voice echoed in his mind.

You were never meant for godhood anyway.

He couldn't help but agree. He glanced back over the city, back to where his companions were shuffling and dealing and losing money that wasn't theirs. He should have felt something. The weight of failure, the violation of breaking the rules that he'd clung to for so long, the promise of something more. But he felt nothing. Only relief.

The Coyote turned and walked on, and he followed.

THE FORTUNE OF SANTOS
EDMOND A PORTER

Once, Alex Turner's career had flared like a supernova, the brightest star in Apex Financials' universe of cosmic luminescence, the best negotiator of his generation. And then it was over, burned out in a sudden blinding flash. The other investment bankers avoided him like he was a black hole, threatening to pull them into the same swirling vortex. To top it off, Susan, his society girlfriend, unable to bear the shame, ejected him like a comet flung out of the solar system by a gravitational slingshot.

His stomach churned as the elevator doors opened on the thirtieth floor. The air felt charged as if the remnants of his galactic downfall lingered. Directly in front of him, a brass plaque identified the office of the CEO, Norman Arnold. He adjusted his tie, crossed the hall, and, with a deep swallow, pushed open the glass door.

"Good afternoon, Mr. Turner," a perky receptionist said,

her smile too bright for Alex's mood. "Have a seat. Mr. Arnold will be right with you."

Alex smiled weakly at the unfamiliar dark-haired woman, guessing she was a temp. He sat uneasily on the hard plastic chair, which was designed for its aesthetic appeal rather than comfort. But he had not expected comfort, as he was certain he would be terminated.

He could see it now: HR representatives demanding his cell phone and ID card, security escorting him from the building with his meager belongings in a cardboard box pilfered from the breakroom, snuffing out his career.

"Mr. Arnold will see you now," the young woman said, her voice far too saccharine for the circumstances.

Alex stood, smoothed the wrinkles from his jacket, and strode down the wood-paneled hallway under the gaze of portraits of CEOs past. If he were going out, at least he'd go with his head held high.

Mr. Arnold stood. "Come in, Alex. Take a seat."

Alex sank into the soft leather chair where he'd sat three years earlier when Arnold had offered him the position. He tried to read the CEO's tone, but it was devoid of any emotion. An open file lay on the desk, but he couldn't read that either.

"Alex," Norman Arnold said. He stood and, picking up the file, walked around the massive walnut desk. He sat on the edge, leaning forward, his face only inches from Alex's. He fingered a note written on distinctive feminine stationery attached to the file; a looping "J" monogram graced the corner. "When was the last time you took an extended vacation?"

"What?" Alex stammered. No one in the business took vacations. Too much could happen in two or three days, let alone weeks.

Arnold repeated himself. "When was your last vacation?"

"I took a long weekend two months ago," Alex said, his voice growing defensive. The weekend visiting his parents in Wyoming had been a disaster. His mother talked of nothing but his breakup with Susan and the possibility of a reunion. His father begged him to return to the ranch. Neither would happen. Susan had moved on, and he'd spent years breaking ties with that forsaken chunk of ground.

The CEO leaned back and folded his arms across his chest. "I'm giving you a six-week leave of absence. I don't want to see or hear from you until the first of March."

Alex's mouth dropped open. He closed it, working his jaws to speak. But no words came out.

"I expect a rejuvenated broker when you come back. Now go before I change my mind."

Alex exited the office and trudged down the hallway, passing the receptionist in a daze, barely acknowledging her cheery, "Have a nice vacation, Mr. Turner."

He'd not expected this outcome. He still had a job. And six weeks of what? He couldn't stay in the city, and he and his parents would tire of each other, or worse, long before six weeks passed. He could spend time with a girlfriend if he still had one, but after Susan, he'd thrown himself deeper into his work for all the good it did him.

He reached the L station on autopilot and boarded without thought. The click-clack of the rails and the crowding passengers felt distant, almost abstract.

An hour later, he unlocked the apartment door, his brain still in a fog. He nuked a frozen dinner and ate it standing at the kitchen island. He tossed the plastic tray into the trash and collapsed onto the sofa in front of the television, promptly falling asleep while a game show played.

The television was still on when he awoke, casting a flickering light across the darkened room. He rubbed his eyes and reached for the remote.

"Come to Santos, Brazil," a woman in a white bikini beckoned. Her sun-kissed skin glowed under the tropical sun, and her long, dark hair flowed gently in a light breeze, framing a face as perfect and captivating as the full moon on a clear night. There was something vaguely familiar about her, though he was certain he'd have remembered meeting someone like her. Behind her, a beautiful sandy beach stretched endlessly; the golden grains of sand sparkled like diamonds in the sun. The blue water rolled in gentle, hypnotic waves.

"Santos is a vibrant city known for its luxurious beaches, bustling port, and rich history," she continued, her voice as inviting as the scenery. The camera panned, capturing the lively streets, the enchanting beach gardens, and smiling locals before focusing on the woman again. "Don't wait. Book your vacation to Santos by scanning the QR code on your screen."

Alex stared at the woman on the television; her broad smile seemed directed at him. He jerked back, his heart skipping a beat. Certainly, she'd only smiled for the camera, but the impression that she was looking directly into his soul lingered, unsettling him. He scanned the QR code with his phone as the television screen suddenly went black. He must have been dreaming, but he was awake. He was sure of that, and the open web page on his phone confirmed it.

He stared at his phone for a moment, the glow dimming as the battery-saver feature kicked in. Sighing, he dropped the phone on the coffee table and headed to bed. But sleep eluded him. Frustrated, he tossed the blanket aside and padded to the living room, drawn by a magnetic pull he couldn't explain. He unlocked his phone, and the website sprang to life.

His breath caught when he saw the forms already populated with his name, address, passport number, and credit card information. His heart raced as his fingers hovered over the phone. He blinked twice, waiting for hesitation to kick in. It didn't. He clicked "Confirm." Within minutes, an email notification pinged, confirming an airline ticket to Sao Paulo and a bus pass to Santos. Only then did buyer's remorse set in.

———

Four days later, Alex stepped off the bus in Santos. Warm, humid air swept over him, a stark contrast to the January snowstorm he'd left behind in Chicago. He was relieved to see a word he recognized. "Taxi." An arrow pointed to the taxi stand, where a queue of cabs waited. He opened the door of the first one, tossed his bag onto the seat, and climbed in.

"Onde vamos, chefe?" The driver asked when Alex closed

the door. "Where are we going, Boss?" appeared on Alex's phone translator app.

"Sheraton Santos," Alex said.

"Muito bem." The driver pushed down the meter flag, and the taxi lurched into traffic, the sound of honking horns filling the air.

At the hotel, a doorman greeted Alex and opened the door of the building. A bluish-gray and white plush carpet, with a pattern mimicking waves on the beach, extended to the check-in desk. His feet sank into the luxurious pile as he crossed the lobby as if walking through dry sand.

With the aid of his translator app, he checked in and was shown to his room by the bellhop, who insisted on carrying Alex's shoulder bag, most likely hoping the American would give him a big tip. Alex obliged, slipping a Brazilian ten-real note into the young man's hand.

"Obrigado, thank you," the boy said with a grin as he closed the door.

Alex surveyed the room, deemed it sufficient, and dropped into bed, eagerly anticipating tomorrow's visit to the beach he'd seen on television. The idea that being there would connect him to the woman from the ad toyed with him, a tantalizing whisper that lulled him into a deep sleep.

———

Sunlight filtered through the blinds, and Alex stretched himself awake, refreshed, having slept better than he had in months, maybe even years. After showering, he unzipped his duffel and dumped his newly purchased wardrobe onto the bed. Tags fluttered from the casual clothes as they landed. This was no place for neckties and Arrow shirts.

He clipped the tags and donned a pair of dark turquoise board shorts, slipping a multi-colored beach shirt featuring a tropical motif over his bare chest. He strapped on a pair of leather sandals and opened the door, ready for the day. It was only two blocks to the beach, and the screech of the gulls and the smell of the salt air assailed him as soon as he left the hotel.

The sand was hot even through the soles of his sandals, prompting him to head for the water, eager for its cool relief, but he stopped short. A woman jogged along the beach. The sun glinted off her tan skin, contrasting with her white bikini.

His heart skipped a beat. For a moment, he thought she was the woman from the television commercial. But as she drew closer, he realized his mistake. Her skin was wrinkled from years of exposure to the sun, and her hair was a dirty blond, not the dark, lustrous locks he remembered. Disappointment washed over him, and he felt foolish for letting his imagination run wild.

With a resigned shake of his head, he continued to the water, took off his sandals, and stepped into the waves. The warm water lapped at his ankles, offering a small comfort. The beach was still beautiful, but the magic he'd hoped to find eluded him.

After an hour of walking on the beach, a burning sensation spread over his arms and neck. Glancing down, he saw that his arms had turned an angry red. He'd been in the tropical sun too long without sunscreen, and it had taken its toll.

He realized he'd also neglected to bring a water bottle. Queasiness swept over him. He needed shade and water, fast.

He gathered his things and stumbled across the soft sand toward the farmácia he remembered passing earlier, hoping they had Aloe Vera. The thought of its cool, soothing gel brought a glimmer of hope.

"Hey, sir. You look like you need water."

Alex heard the words but couldn't see the speaker through his narrowing vision. Then darkness closed around him, and he collapsed onto the hot sand.

He awoke in the farmácia, seated in an unstable wooden chair. The room spun. He squeezed his eyes closed.

"Good. You're awake," someone said. It sounded like the voice he'd heard on the beach, but, in his current state, he couldn't be sure.

Alex forced his eyes open. His vision was blurred, but he could barely discern a woman holding a water bottle. She placed the bottle next to Alex's lips.

He grabbed the bottle and gulped.

"Slow down," she said. "You'll make yourself sick."

Alex sipped the water and felt a little strength returning. He lifted his clouded eyes to her. "You speak English."

"Yes. My father works in international trade. I'm here to visit my parents."

Alex cursed his blurry vision. He couldn't accurately discern her features, but her voice seemed kind and caring, almost familiar. Beyond her immediate concern for his well-being, he sensed her excitement about visiting her parents; after all, why not? It was Santos, Brazil, not Podunk, Wyoming.

"Do you need help?" she asked. "I'll get my friends to assist you." She motioned to the street where several people milled about.

"No. I'll be fine." Alex stood, and the room swayed.

She reached out to steady him, her touch warm and soothing. He didn't want her to go, not really, but he gave a slight wave that said he'd be all right on his own.

"Nice meeting you, Alex," she said as she turned and walked out of the farmácia, joining her friends.

Alex watched her go, his memory as hazy as his vision. He didn't remember telling the woman his name, yet she'd called him Alex. He must have said something. Maybe she'd looked at his ID, but it was in the wallet zippered in his pocket. Or was this just another detail blurred by fatigue and sunstroke? He shook his head and crossed to the counter.

After purchasing a bottle of aloe to treat his sunburn and resting long enough for his vision to return, he exited the farmácia and turned toward the hotel. He'd walked only a short distance when a brightly lit shop caught his eye. The shop's façade was adorned with colorful, flickering lights. Beads hung across the doorway, shimmering in the glow of dozens of candles. The candles, mostly melted to waxy puddles, adorned the sidewalk with blue, green, and red splotches. A tall white candle extended above the others, its wick burning a bright orange yet showing no signs of melting.

Intrigued, Alex stepped closer, his eyes drawn to the candle like a bee to nectar. He squatted down and touched the candle, doubting it could be made of wax. The moment his fingers touched the candle, the beads rustled, and a dark-haired woman dressed in a gaudy, multi-colored dress stepped out. Her eyes flashed with a knowing spark, and a faint, enigmatic smile played on her lips.

"Can I help you?" she asked in heavily accented English.

Alex jumped to his feet, unable to speak a word.

"You must come in and get your palm read," she said.

"Another time," Alex managed to say. He turned to walk away, but she caught him by the arm and pulled him through the colorful curtain, the beads clicking noisily against one another.

"Sit," she commanded, her tone so sharp that Alex sat.

His eyes surveyed the room. A flashing neon sign behind her proclaimed, "Señora Isabela, Fortune Teller." Flames danced from rows of candles, and the aroma of incense filled the space. Tarot cards lay on the table to his right. And a colorful hen huddled in the corner of an intricate wooden cage, emitting a single cluck as Alex sat. He'd heard about rituals in Brazil, where macumbeira offered colorful poultry as a sacrifice to induce spells, but this was evidence that such practices could be real. Could their magic be real as well? A shiver ran down his spine despite the oppressive heat. He struggled to stand, but the woman held his arm tightly, fixing him in place.

"Give me your palm, and I will tell you your future," Isabela said, her accent so thick Alex could barely understand.

Alex resisted, but the woman gripped his hand firmly and turned it over. His clenched fist opened involuntarily under her touch, as if she had some power he couldn't resist.

She studied Alex's hand for several minutes. Occasionally, a hem, haw, or humph escaped her lips, but she said nothing.

The sunburn on Alex's arms and neck grew painful as the effects of the aloe wore off. He shifted in his chair, coiling his legs beneath him, ready to spring away if Isabela loosened her grip. But her hold tightened as she ran her index finger along the lines of his palm.

"You have a strong fate line." Her voice grew lower in tone, almost forced. "I sense you seek a dangerous fortune."

She released his hand, and he jumped to his feet, staggering through the beaded curtain and into the street. The sun had already set, leaving behind ominous shadows. The music of street musicians drifted from the beach gardens, their haunting samba rhythms weaving through the air and fueling the foreboding that settled over him. The scent of seawater mingled with the aroma of grilled meat from the nearby churrascaria, but he barely noticed, his mind consumed by the strange encounter.

His latest slump notwithstanding, he had grossed a tidy sum in his three years at Apex and knew he could earn much more. Of course, the fortune teller could see it in his fate line; even Arnold had seen it. Why else had he given him a leave of absence instead of firing him? But Isabela's warning of danger pushed those thoughts aside.

———

Back in his hotel room, Alex slathered aloe gel onto his neck and arms, sighing with relief at the soothing effect. He fell into bed, exhausted, sleeping fitfully. His encounter with the palm reader infiltrated his dreams and overshadowed his collapse from dehydration. He awoke early and then dressed, unwilling to spend his time inside a hotel room, no matter how grand it was.

He grabbed a muffin and a cup of yogurt from the hotel's breakfast buffet before walking to the beach, this time slathered in sunscreen and carrying a water bottle. Gulls played tag with the waves, and he watched them until he grew bored; then he ventured to the Orla do Santos. The hotel brochure described it as a seven-kilometer-long promenade stretching from São Vicente to Ponta da Praia. It was all that, packed with cafés, shops, and even a movie theater. Statues of historic figures and bike and skating paths added to its charm.

He strolled toward Ponta da Praia, enjoying the gentle breeze blowing across the bay. Shouts of excitement from a soccer game drifted from the beach. Futebol, he reminded himself as he strolled in the game's direction, drawn by a sudden urge to explore the enthusiasm.

"Come play with us," one of the players called over the rhythmic sound of the waves.

Alex looked over his shoulder to see who the player was inviting. No one was behind him. He pointed his finger at his chest, his eyebrows raised in question.

"Yes, you," the player said.

Alex shrugged and walked across the sand to where the man stood with his arm wrapped around a tattered soccer ball. "Are you sure you want me to play?" he asked.

"It's Americans against Brazilians, and we're getting creamed. You play, don't you?"

Alex looked at the team lined up across the crudely organized pitch. His eyes opened wide. The Brazilian squad
consisted of mere boys, the oldest of whom appeared to be
about twelve years old.

"Yes, but I haven't played in years," Alex said.

"Close enough; I'm only part American," the player whispered as if divulging a deep secret. He dropped the ball to the
sand and dribbled toward the opposing team.

During a break in the game, Alex approached the player
he'd learned was named Lucas. "How did you know I was
American?"

"I helped get you to the farmácia last night," Lucas said.

"Thank you. I appreciate your help." Alex's face reddened
as he remembered the embarrassing circumstances.

Lucas shrugged. "No problem. It was Julianna's idea;
there's no changing her mind when it is set on something."

"You seem to know a lot about her. Is she your girlfriend?" Alex asked.

Lucas laughed—not a full, carefree sound but one clipped
and uneven. "No. She's my sister. At least, I think she still is. She's
been...different lately. Almost like she's only partially herself."

Alex detected a tremble in Lucas's voice. Was it worry?
He opened his mouth to ask what Lucas meant, but thought
better of it. He didn't want to get involved in another family's
drama. He had enough of his own.

"Sem essa? Vamos jogar," the tallest of the Brazilian
players called impatiently.

"It looks like time out is over," Lucas said, running across
the sand, kicking up a spray of golden particles.

———

"Thanks for inviting me to play," Alex said after the game. "It was fun even though we lost badly."

"It was," Lucas said, brushing sand from his shirt. He paused for a moment as if undecided about his following words, then went on. "Some friends are getting together at the nightclub tonight. You should come. I'd like you to meet my sister properly. She is the one who insisted on helping you after all."

"Sure," Alex said.

While he was only focused on meeting one woman in Santos—the model from the television ad—he wouldn't turn down the opportunity to meet someone who had been so kind to him.

"Give me your phone number, and I'll text you the details."

After exchanging contact information with Lucas, Alex left the beach and ambled down the promenade to the Municipal Aquarium. It was not a large exhibit, with only a few sharks, some playful seals, and several tanks of tropical fish. There was something relaxing about this city, and he seemed to have fallen under its charm. He hadn't thought about the "dangerous fortune" all day until he turned a corner and came face-to-face with a piranha tank. The sharp-toothed predator fish stared at him through the glass, their cold, calculating eyes reminding him of Isabela. He shuddered at the memory. At that moment, his phone buzzed with a text—*Santorini's at eight.*

————

"Glad you could make it," Lucas said, grabbing Alex by the elbow. "Most of the group is inside."

A soft red glow from above the bar was the only light, and it took a moment for Alex's eyes to adjust, but the steady pressure of Lucas's hand on his elbow kept him moving forward.

"Everyone, this is Alex. Alex, this is everyone," Lucas said over the loud, pulsing music.

The five people seated at the table offered greetings, most of which were in Portuguese. Alex fumbled with his phone to open the translator app.

"I'll translate for you," Lucas said.

"Are all your friends Brazilian?"

"All except my sister, Julianna. She's only partly Brazilian, like me. She should be here any minute. Let me introduce you to everyone." He pointed to the person to his left. "This is Pedro and his girlfriend, Maria Gracia. Then, Rafael, Beatriz, and Celia."

With formalities out of the way, the group chatted over food and drinks while Lucas translated. Alex offered little to the conversation, but learned that Pedro had grown up in Santos and had met Maria Gracia at university, where she studied engineering. Rafael was an accomplished guitarist, and Beatriz and Celia were secretaries working for Lucas and Julianna's father. Lucas, like Julianna, was visiting. He lived in New York.

Alex couldn't help noticing how often Lucas checked his

phone and glanced at the door. "Is something wrong?" he asked, leaning close to Lucas.

"Julianna is late. It's not like her." Lucas's voice trembled as he rechecked the time, his fingers jittering over the phone screen.

"Is there something I can do?" Alex asked.

Before Lucas could answer, they were interrupted by a movement at the other end of the table.

Pedro stood, offering his hand to Maria Gracia and helping her from the chair. "Excuse us. We must leave," he said in broken English.

The others, as if taking Pedro's hint, all murmured their regrets and left the nightclub, like Julianna's continued absence created some cosmic shift.

"Let me help you find your sister," Alex said as soon as they were alone at the table. "Do you have any idea where to start looking?"

Lucas nodded. "Let's get out of here," he shouted over the pulsating rhythm of the band that had just started playing.

They left the nightclub, the harsh neon lights on the exterior preventing Alex from seeing Lucas's face, and the pounding of the music making communication difficult. They made their way down the street, stopping under a streetlight near a bus stop.

Lucas cleared his throat. "Did you know that Julianna brought you here?"

"But she didn't even come to the nightclub."

"I mean, she brought you to Brazil."

Alex stared at Lucas without comprehension. "No. I came

because I had a six-week leave of absence and nowhere to go."

"Do you remember the temp at Arnold's office?"

Alex's gaze jerked toward Lucas. "How do you know about her? And what does that have to do with your sister?" But even as he asked the question, the image of the feminine stationery attached to his file flickered through his mind.

"And the TV ad?" Lucas asked.

"What?" Alex asked. Lucas could not know those things. He'd told no one. "That was merely a coincidence. I needed somewhere to go, and the ad prompted me to come to Brazil. It could have been anywhere." Yet, the churning in his gut told him that was not true.

Lucas's eyes narrowed. "Julianna was searching for help, and she'd seen your profile in a financial magazine. The reporter called you the brightest star in Apex Financial's universe, the man who could negotiate a deal with the devil."

Alex remembered that interview. The reporter had followed him around for a week, right before the implosion that sent his life spiraling out of control.

"She was convinced you could help her resolve an issue she was having with a certain fortune teller who divided her."

"The fortune teller made your sister doubt herself?"

"No. She actually split her into three. Three parts of herself."

Alex wanted to object that such a thing was impossible. But the fortune teller's flashing eyes filled his mind, and he remembered the command in her voice that he hadn't been able to resist. He shuddered. Somehow, he knew it was true.

"I know who you mean. I had an encounter with Isabela myself. Do you think she has Julianna?"

"I'm certain."

"Then let's go," Alex said.

Lucas's eyes widened. "I can't go there," he moaned. "Isabela has cursed me for trying to help Julianna before."

"You can't abandon your sister."

"You don't understand. I physically cannot go there. Isabela's curse blocks me from her physical presence."

"How much power does this woman have?" Alex asked.

"Way more than you can imagine. But not as much as she could have, if Julianna had not intervened."

Alex shuddered. "That is why she has cursed Julianna?

Lucas nodded.

Alex collapsed on the bench at the bus stop, thoughts of the influence Isabela had, keeping him in her shop against his will, rippling over him. The candles, tarot cards, and colorful caged bird were no longer merely suggestions of magical power, but proof. How could he go up against such a powerful sorceress? The word caused gooseflesh to ripple across his body, but at the same time, he thought of the perky receptionist, the beautiful model, and the kind-hearted woman who'd given him water. He clenched his fists. He had to try.

A red and grey bus rattled to a stop, and Alex boarded with a glance back at Lucas, yearning for his company.

"Good luck," Lucas called weakly as the bus pulled away.

Alex paid the conductor and moved to the front of the bus. Then, as suddenly and unexpectedly as a meteor streaking across the night sky, Alex stood outside the fortune teller's shop. He pushed through the beads and stood along-side three familiar women in the fortune teller's shop. Seeing them together—the receptionist, the model, and the kind stranger—it seemed obvious that they were part of the whole. From the surprise on the women's faces, he realized that they'd been transported here, and it was as startling to them as it was to him.

Isabela stepped close to Alex, her eyes sweeping across the three women. "Did you find your fortune?"

Alex positioned himself between Isabela and the women with more bravado than he felt. "I've come to claim my fortune."

Isabela's cold, mocking gaze fell on Alex. "Do you think you can thwart me? The last time I saw you, you were nothing but a sunburned, sniveling coward who couldn't wait to get away." She turned to the women. "What do you think of your foreigner now? You brought him here because you thought he was so clever, but as you can see, he is nothing, just like your worthless brother."

"I am prepared to negotiate," Alex said, drawing himself up to his full height. He towered over Isabela, but his height gave him little assurance against her magic.

"What do you have to negotiate with?"

Alex swallowed hard. "My wits."

Isabela threw back her head and cackled. "Your wits against my magic."

"You can give up if you think you're overmatched."

"If you are so smart, try this," Isabela sneered. "One in this shop holds your fortune. If you choose correctly, it's yours. If you make the wrong choice, you, the fortune, the hapless brother, and the women will be gone forever."

Alex's blood ran cold. "What if I don't choose?" he asked, his voice trembling.

"There must be a choice." Isabela's eyes were as cold as the piranhas'.

"Why?"

Isabela's voice turned even more sinister. "Julianna destroyed a powerful artifact that would have ensured my reign as supreme macumbeira. To exact my revenge, I split her into three. If you don't make a choice, she will remain in her current state forever."

The room closed around Alex. If he didn't break Isabela's spell, he, Julianna, and Lucas were doomed to extinction. His eyes darted from one woman to the next, each face reflecting a different aspect of what she might be, yet there was no light in their eyes, no signal of who was the embodiment of the real soul.

His mind raced. What if he made the wrong choice? The beads clacking in the breeze and the hen clucking in the cage across the room rattled his thoughts. Sweat beaded on his forehead and trickled down his back. His eyes flicked to the caged fowl, no longer huddling in the corner but strutting boldly around the inside of the cage, its fussing growing louder and more agitated. Did it know it was supposed to be used to feed or bribe a spirit?

Isabela's words became clear. One in this room held his fortune, not one woman, but one entity. Desperation surged through him; he made his decision. He rushed across the shop and ripped open the cage. Grabbing the bird, he sprinted through the beads and into the street.

A blood-curdling scream sounded behind him, and he turned as Isabela's shop dissolved into a puff of smoke, leaving only one flickering candle as a sign of its existence and its former occupants.

Alex stood alone, holding the near-lifeless fowl in his arms. The silence of the night was broken only by the distant crash of waves like a samba rhythm faintly echoing from nowhere. His heart shattered into a million pieces.

"I chose wrong," he cried into the night air as he slumped to the ground.

He'd been as sure of his decision as any he'd ever made, but he'd been wrong, again.

He had gambled everything. The night air mocked him. He wanted to scream, to vanish, to undo the moment. But the bird stirred, fluttering from his hands, shimmering upward in the streetlight. As it ascended, its plumage began to phosphoresce, sending out streamers of brilliant greens, blues, and reds. Its body elongated, taking on a human form, with its wings morphing into slender arms, and its head transforming into delicate features. The beautiful woman from the beach settled to the ground before him; her kindly smile was nearly too bright, a perfect blend of the three women.

"Thank you for saving me and my brother," Julianna whispered. "I was scattered across space, but even with each part of me holding a different fear, I knew you could do it."

"How did you know?"

Julianna's eyes sparkled. "They said you could negotiate

with the devil, and I could see into your soul and knew it was true," she said.

Near the vanished shop, the lone candle flared briefly, casting a shadow slithering across the pavement before dropping back to a mere flicker, barely noticeable.

Julianna took his hand as a fireball streaked across the sky, exploding into a thousand shimmering sparks of color that illuminated the way ahead. His steps felt lighter as if gravity had shifted as they made their way to the beach, where Lucas stood waiting for them.

10

THE DELIVERY

K.G. MONTGOMERY

I didn't think the wasp would have time to sting, but I guess that's what I get for doing a reactionary smash just as it landed on my computer desk. Plus, serves me right for leaving my apartment window open to the fire escape. At least it wasn't a rat.

The sharp pain in my palm morphs into a throbbing. I pull the tiny stinger from my skin and stare at my first mistake of the day, and I'm barely post breakfast.

"Andrew, did you just kill a bug in the middle of our morning meeting?" My supervisor, Stan, is squinting from his thumbnail on my computer screen.

The best way to describe my impression of Stan, and one that would be HR-approved if my inner thoughts ever became impulsive outer ones, is: *He has a unique way of motivating the team*. In truth, I loathe him and his smirking face whenever he's pawning his tasks onto others. Mostly, I loathe that he's related to the CEO.

Stan starts tapping his microphone as if he's thumping the top of my head. "Can ... you ... hear ... me?"

My hand hurts, and there's a dead wasp smeared on the fake wood grain of my second-hand desk.

"Andrew!"

I shake the camera that's perched on my monitor. "Bad connection, Stan. Better email me the rest of the presentation."

"But, Andrew, you're my point-man. I need you to finish my—"

I push *leave meeting*, and I'm gone.

Now, I can breathe.

I stand to stretch, still nursing my burning palm, and free the loose tie from my half-buttoned white dress shirt. When both it and the shirt hit the floor and my skin is bare, all that's left is the flannel pajama pants I've worn for three days straight. There's no need to change them because I work remote. And since Trisha moved out a month ago, it takes convincing to even shower on a regular basis.

At the sudden thought of her, a heaviness grows in my head and chest—one that's been entrenching itself whenever I recall the left-over echo of her slamming the door that one last time.

I kick a shoe against the wall, then blank-stare at my messy couch, trying to push the memory of Trisha from my mind.

Whatever.

I slump down on the couch with a groan, feet up, throbbing hand on a pillow, and pick at the leftovers of the latest middle-of-the-night Chinese food delivery that I forgot to put in the fridge. The city stinks in general, but the option of 24-hour food delivery is a staple in my new hermit lifestyle.

I stir the noodles a bit, then take a bite. It tastes like dried-out insomnia and impulsivity.

"Ugh." I toss the container down on the coffee table next to an old pizza box. My core feels heavy again, but at least I have groceries coming this afternoon as a distraction.

What's next? Nap? Or shower? I shake my head. *Or...*

A sudden knock at the door breaks my train of thought.

Whoa, that was quick. Groceries usually don't arrive until after three.

I hurry over to the door and spy through the peephole, ready to pretend I'm not home until after the delivery guy leaves.

But the hallway is empty.

I squint into the circle, as if that will improve the view through the distorted fish-eye lens. Still nobody. The grocery guy usually waits for a moment before he gives up and abandons the order, so it can't be early groceries. My lips tighten, and a nervous, burning sensation percolates in my stomach —one matching the burning wasp sting in my palm.

With caution, I open the door a crack, leaving the chain still attached, and peer through the slit. Everything seems ordinary, and the hallway's quiet. But as I scan down, I spot a brown package on my doorstep that I don't remember ordering. It's square. Small. Addressed in permanent marker letters that I can't quite make out from my angle.

I unlock, grab, and shut in one fell swoop. The box is now in my hand and the door is locked again. I take the package over to my desk and set it gently in the center, a ridiculous scenario popping into my head of when movie characters open a package only to find an unexploded bomb inside and a countdown clock heading to zero. *Am I supposed to cut the red wire or avoid it? Do I even own wire-cutters?*

I scoff at myself. Too many 3 A.M. movies.

Moving on. The package's mailing address consists of scratchy, hand-written letters that spell out my building, but the apartment number is smeared a bit. It looks like my *#403* before it was defiled by the smudge. No postage, as if delivered directly from the sender, which is listed as *Victor's Game Emporium*—a place I didn't know existed.

I step back and stare down at the package, deciding what to do.

Screw it. I rip open the outer brown parcel paper and find a plain inner box, no markings, deep blue in color, with a simple lid that comes off easily. Inside, I find tissue paper wrapped around a . . .

My whole face tightens in confusion.

In the center of the tissue padding is a light switch in a switch plate. Not the simple plastic kind I have on my wall, which turns the lights on and off, but one made of antique brass with a central toggle that has a small ball on the end. The brass plate is backed with another metal box to house it instead of the standard loose connecting wires. The plate itself has small swooping leaf designs on the surface with the words *ON* and *OFF* in block letters above and below the central toggle.

My face gets even tighter as I hold it in my hand, the cold metal from the switch's box cooling my wasp sting. I've never seen a light switch like this one before, and I can't figure out why a game emporium and not a hardware store would have one, let alone send it to me.

Whatever.

I shrug and casually flip the toggle to ON with my thumb.

An electric shock zaps my palm and fingers, accompanied by a crackling sound.

"Ah!"

I drop the switch. The shock is quick, intense, like touching a doorknob after building up a ton of static in your socks.

It takes me a few seconds to settle my breathing and heart rate. I eye the switch on the wooden floor without moving, as if expecting it to bite me. When I collect myself, I take stock of my hand. It doesn't seem to hurt anymore, and the wasp sting is . . . *gone.*

As in, my skin is smooth and flat like the sting never happened.

My eyes grow wide, and I rub my palm over and over again in disbelief. *No way. There's no way this is real.*

I pick up the switch by its corner, minimal contact, and set it on my desk with care. Then I riffle through the delivery box again, this time finding an enclosed folded paper that looks at first glance like some kind of invoice. It reads:

Included as ordered: One Fix-It-Switch. Read all directions before use.

1. Place switch on desired object for repair. Ensure direct contact.

2. Turn toggle to ON. Allow a few seconds for the fix-it task to be completed.

3. Ensure that the Fix-It-Switch has turned itself into the OFF position before attempting another task.

4. Do not submerge in water.

For troubleshooting, contact Victor at Victor's Game Emporium.

At the bottom of the page is a phone number. I flip the paper around and search the backside for more information, but there is none.

This can't be all of it. Where is the explanation on how this kind of thing even happens—witchcraft or lasers or aliens? I feel like I'm going crazy.

I hurry over to my computer and type the name of the store into the search bar. Nothing directly related comes up —no address, no website, no social media page, only an obscure chat forum with a comment that mentions how "Victor has a way with magic" before they start talking about collecting objects for some game. The details are vague and don't make any sense to me. The forum conversation itself is short. And old.

I give up and glance at the Fix-It-Switch waiting with such innocence on my desk. For the second time today, I realize I made a mistake. The directions said to read them all before use, which, of course, I didn't because I didn't bother to even look inside the rest of the box. I need to be more careful.

So, I sit still and do what I should have done before—

slow down, contemplate, and work towards deciding how I want to handle this unknown thing from a stranger who *has a way with magic*, as if that's even possible and . . .

Forget it. I jump up and grab the switch, spinning around in search of something to use this thing on.

The Chinese Food. I kneel down next to the coffee table and shove the switch into the container so the backside is pressed against the stringy noodles.

I flip the toggle to *ON*.

This time, I don't feel the electric shock, but I hear the surge like a crackling whip. The dried-out food softens before my eyes and comes back to life as if it's being served directly from the wok. The toggle flips itself to *OFF*.

I wipe the food sauce residue from the backplate onto my pants and lean down to study the noodles.

Looks good.

With bravery, I grab a long noodle and coil it into my mouth. The day-old ick is gone, and it tastes fresh like amazing possibilities.

I lean back with the switch in my hand, heart and mind racing, and an excitement fills my core that I haven't felt in months. The thing works. The forum was right. Whoever Victor is, he *does* have a way with magic. I can't believe it, but I'll take it.

Find more things.

There are so many broken and neglected items in my apartment that my mind spins with what to fix next, and then my gaze catches on the crumpled brown paper that the box came in and the smudged address. With care, I set the switch on top of the marker smear. I toggle *ON*.

After the familiar crackle, the toggle flips itself to *OFF*. I raise the switch to see the outcome. My heart sinks. The apartment number has been restored, but it doesn't say my *#403*. It reads *#408*. The delivery was a mistake, meant for one of my neighbors. I feel . . . *low* again.

The disappointment is understandable, but I'm not sure why I'm surprised considering I'm a voluntary recluse. Besides Stan and "the team" of thumbnail faces, my apartment is self-contained, isolated, and I've been interacting with no one. It's quiet, except for the ceiling fan that wobbles and hums. Of course, there's overlapping city noises that waft in from my open window—reminding me that I'm one of eight million even though I'm not really one of them.

And I can't escape the muffled sounds of my apartment neighbors, their noisy lives seeping in through unseen cracks in my safe haven until I unwillingly know the inner workings of behind their closed doors. Upstairs, the guy drinks in the evenings until clanking bottles get dropped on the wooden floor. To my right, they fight. And make up. And fight again. Sometimes it's bad. I hear more than I want to, which I wish was none.

To my left, the old lady leaves the TV running all day and night ever since her husband died. One of her adult kids comes a lot. I hear him in the hallway almost every morning, though I haven't today, and she's been quiet.

No one would send me such a thing as a magical do-over that lets you repair what's broken. Where would I even start?

I cradle the switch in my hands, knowing my time with it is limited. No more fixing old food and smudges. I need to think bigger.

As fast as I can go, I shower, dress, and then stash the Fix-It-Switch in my jacket pocket as I exit my apartment. I glance left and right down the hallway, deciding what to do next.

The old lady.

I knock on door #401 and ignore the nerves percolating in my stomach.

She opens it but leaves the chain connected. "Yes?"

Her eyes look tired, and she's wearing a heavy sweater that's too thick for the season. I can't remember her name, Susan or Sharon maybe.

"Hi . . . I'm Andrew. I don't know if you remember me, but I'm the guy who lives next door."

She squints over her reading glasses. "Oh, right. Didn't recognize you with that messy beard." She shuts the door, fiddles with the chain, then opens it wide. "What happened to you, Andrew? You look like a mountain man."

"I've been working from home. I guess I don't get out much."

"Oh." She stares at me for a moment. "I know how that is. Anyway, how's Trisha? She hasn't come over to help me with a crossword puzzle in a while."

I scrunch my brow. "She used to come here?"

"Sometimes. Started after my Ralph died, rest his soul, but I haven't seen her since last month."

"I didn't know Trisha did that."

She nods and gives me a polite smile.

I feel heavy again, but I don't let myself walk away. Instead, I remember the Fix-It-Switch waiting in my pocket. "Um, is there anything that you need help with?" My words come out stiff. "I'm not good at crosswords, but maybe I could . . . fix something." I hold my breath and ride out the awkwardness.

She glances behind her into the apartment. "Well, my TV just died. Probably used it too much. It fills up the quiet. My son is going to buy me a new one when he gets paid."

"Can I take a look at it?"

"I guess. But my son says it's a goner."

"That's okay."

She shows me inside to where a small, dark TV is resting atop a kitchen table. There are several medicine bottles in a grouping near the center and a place-setting for one person. I tilt my head and glance fast at the name on one of the bottles —Sylvia.

The room smells like she's cooking on the stove, and I realize that my 6-foot-tall body is taking up a lot of space in the narrow gaps between the oversized, antique furniture.

"You're welcome to it, Andrew," Sylvia says, and goes back to the kitchen.

I pretend to inspect the TV for a moment, making sure her attention is elsewhere. Then I pull the switch from my pocket and hold it against the black screen.

While listening to her hum from the kitchen, I steady myself and toggle the switch to *ON*.

Crackle.

The television comes to life, a game show filling the screen, and seconds later, the toggle flips to *OFF*.

"Oh! You got it working again!" She hurries over from the stove and pats me on the arm.

I stash the switch in my pocket, feeling relieved. "Yep. No problem, Sylvia."

"I'll call my son. Thank you, Andrew!"

I nod and smile, then start shuffling my way around the antique furniture towards the door.

"Will you come by with Trisha next time?" she calls after me.

I stop short. And sigh. "We're not together anymore."

Sylvia frowns and tilts her head. "Oh, Andrew. I'm so sorry to hear that. Well, whatever went wrong, just do what you can to fix it."

I don't know how to respond. So, I nod again and make my way outside into the hallway. "See you later."

With that, I leave her smiling and waving goodbye as she closes the door.

I pace down the hall, my mind racing on a thousand things, like how it actually felt good to fix the TV, and wondering if I could even do crosswords . . . I pause mid-stride after realizing I'm passing apartment #408. I blank-stare at the door's peephole and brass numbers, my racing thoughts coming to a halt on one sentence that echoes loud in my brain—the package was meant for 408. Then, as if overwriting the thought, I remember Sylvia's words telling me to fix the problem with Trisha.

I grip the Fix-It-Switch in my pocket. I need more time.

Clinking sounds spike my adrenaline. The door-knob and chain inside 408 begin to jingle.

Without thinking, I bolt down the hallway towards the stairs before the door has time to fully open. I reach the stairwell at full sprint and clomp down on the lower landing just as I hear the reverberating echo of 408's door slamming shut. Then there's fast stomping steps on the hard floor above me.

I practically fly down the next set of stairs, full panic, not looking back, and clear the three remaining flights until I exit into the lobby, my out-of-shape lungs wheezing. People in the room startle at my sudden appearance. There's a man getting his mail from the boxes on the wall, and a woman with a leashed dog is standing in front of the main entrance. Behind me, the swift footsteps are coming down the stairwell. I run, dodge, weave, and ignore the barking until I'm out on the city street and am bombarded by the sunlight and the noise.

My senses are overwhelmed, rusty from the month of living indoors. I stagger down the sidewalk and shield my eyes. As they adjust, I concentrate on where I need to go—it's near lunch time, and Trisha always eats at the river-side plaza near her office's complex.

I flag a cab, knowing the subway will take too long, and slide into the back seat as soon as it meets me at the curb. The yellow taxi smells of someone's late night at the club.

"Where to?" the driver asks through the partition. He's a middle-aged guy who looks like he's been sitting in that seat for far too long and is now a vehicle accessory.

"Riverside Plaza South," I say.

"That'll need to be cash. My card reader is broken."

"Okay." I notice the reader's screen in front of me says *ERROR*. Without hesitating, I press the Fix-It-Switch to the card device and toggle it. The crackling sound blends in with the honking and street noise.

In a few seconds, the display changes to *READY* and then flashes: *PAID IN FULL.*

"It might be good now," I say.

The driver glances at his own screen up front. "Yeah, I guess it is. Looks like your card went through. Perfect." He pulls away from the curb.

A thrill washes over me as I realize the switch made the ride free, and for a moment, I forget my urgency.

The feeling lingers as we drive down the city streets, then it's replaced by nerves again when I spot the plaza through the windshield.

"Let me off there." I point to a spot at the curb.

He obeys.

I jump out and sprint into the park, dodging joggers, cyclists, and pigeons until I spot her.

Trisha is sitting and eating her lunch, facing away, just past the main pavilion at a bench near the edge of the canal —her favorite spot. The nearby trees protect her with their shade, and a cool breeze brushes wisps of brown hair around her shoulders as she stares out over the water and towards the tall office buildings across the canal.

I approach, a bit awkward and clunky, and stand next to the bench.

"Hey," I say, realizing I should have planned my words when I was in the cab.

She stares up at me and squints. "Andrew? What are you doing here?"

Good question. I glance at the sky for a second, my heart pounding. "Well, I needed to talk to you. It's been rough since you left. I want to fix things."

Trisha exhales deeply, and her expression sinks. Without saying a word, she packs her lunch into a bag at her side, then stands to face me while pulling the strap over her shoulder.

I breathe shallow while she moves, waiting.

"Andrew, it's been rough for me, too," she says.

"Then come back."

She shakes her head. "I can't go back to the way it was."

"Okay, I get that."

"Do you? Andrew, we've been growing apart for a while, and you know it."

I stare out over her head, fighting the heaviness growing in my rib cage.

"You hate change," she says. "You want everything to stay the same all the time. Same job. Same apartment. Same life. Same old complaints. That's you, but it's not me."

"So, you're still angry about the job offer in Chicago." I meet her eyes again.

Trisha folds her arms. "I'm not angry. I'm hurt. When I got that offer, you didn't even want to talk about it. I'd been waiting for that opportunity for a long time, longer than the two years we were together. Stan lets you work remote from anywhere, but you just dismissed the idea without discussion. Like you didn't even care how much the offer meant to me."

I swallow hard. "I cared. I just . . ." I pause. I don't know what to say. Just like I didn't know what to say on the day she first told me and the day she left, when the thought of starting over somewhere new filled me with dread. Maybe she was right. Maybe I do hate change. Maybe we have grown apart. But . . . maybe it doesn't have to stay that way. I reach my hand into my pocket and grip the switch.

"Why has it taken you a month to come talk to me?" she asks.

I stop short.

"Why today? Why now instead of trying to fix things sometime in the last month, or even earlier than that when we were still together and it was getting hard?"

"It's . . ." my mind is racing, but my words feel stuck, ". . . complicated."

"It isn't." Her voice quivers. "You broke my heart."

"I can fix it."

Trisha glances away into the plaza. "It's not that simple." She lowers her head and closes her eyes.

"Maybe it is." I quickly pull the Fix-It-Switch out of my pocket before she looks up, pressing it to her upper arm and flipping the toggle to *ON*.

I wait for the crackling, my heart racing, but the sound doesn't come.

"What are you doing?" she asks, her eyes open again. "What is that thing?"

"Um." I flip the toggle up and down a few times with it still pressed against her arm, but nothing is changing. As I stare down at the switch, disbelief and panic hit me hard.

"Andrew," Trisha says, stepping out of my reach. "I accepted the job offer. I'm moving to Chicago at the end of the week. I still care about you very much, but we want different things. There's no way to fix that."

I shake the switch in my hand and whack it a few times, frustration taking over.

"Look, I know this stings, but we'll both be okay. It's the right thing for both of us. I wish you the best life. Goodbye,

Andrew." She turns and walks away from the bench, heading towards the pavilion and not looking back.

Goodbye? I whack the switch again. It has to work. It has to! This doesn't make any sense. I glance up and notice Trisha's walking fast and has reached the side of the pavilion.

I step out to follow, tunnel-visioned on her in the distance. "Wait! Just give me a sec—"

Something hits me—hard. I'm pushed back with force, barely catching a glimpse of the cyclist and his bike as they collide with me at full speed. I'm flying backward, feet tripping, and flip over the short metal railing between the edge and the canal.

I fall without control, spinning head-first, and hit the water. It engulfs me quick and cold, shocking my skin. I manage to keep a death grip on the switch, and I whip my arms and legs trying to right myself and surface. My entire body feels heavy and in full panic.

The current is strong. I fight, but I'm not winning.

Seconds later, something grabs my jacket collar and pulls me towards the top. I'm jerked out of the water, gasping, and someone is flopping me over the railing and onto the cement like a fish.

I lay there for a moment, coughing and catching my breath, gripping the switch against my soaked chest. My head is spinning, and every sore and bruised inch of me is dripping on the ground.

"You thought you could swim," a man says in a heavy Russian accent. "Good thing Victor was here to save you." He thumps himself on the chest and gives a hardy belly laugh.

The man leans over me. *Victor* is the size of a bodybuilder, with a bald head and a trimmed beard. He has a full sleeve of tattoos on the arm he used to pull me out of the water, an effort that seemed as simple for him as if he was uncorking a vodka bottle.

"Victor." A woman pushes past him and comes into my view. "Let him breathe." She's tan with long black hair and deep eyes. "Are you okay?"

I nod, even though I'm not really sure.

"There!" Victor says, pointing at my chest. "Your switch, Elena."

I glance down at my hand that's still gripping the metal box, my heart sinking.

They both squat down at my side.

Victor reaches for the switch. I have no choice but to slowly unclench my fingers and let it go.

He takes it and examines the brass, tipping the switch on its side until a stream of water empties out of the backplate and lands on the cement in a tiny puddle. "You know, to submerge in water is bad. I warn."

"That wasn't my plan," I say, sitting up.

"Was it your plan to keep my delivery?" Elena asks. "I'm your neighbor in 408. I almost caught you earlier, but you run fast. It's a good thing that Victor can track his switches. So, what were you trying to do?"

I wipe my face with a wet sleeve. "Fix things with my girl-friend. I mean, my ex-girlfriend. But it didn't work. She's gone."

"Ah," Elena says, shaking her head. "The switch fixes objects—tangible things. Not emotions. Not a broken heart. It can't fix that or make people change their minds."

This hits me hard. Trisha's parting words replay through mind, and I realize I was so focused on making the switch work that I missed my chance to fix anything real. My heart aches. Trisha was right—this does sting. And more than any wasp ever could cause. I feel like I lost her twice.

"Accept fate," Victor says, and he helps me stand.

I nod because he's right. But on the inside, I feel defeated. I stare at the switch in Victor's grip, unsure of what life will be like tomorrow.

"What is it for, really?" I ask.

Victor glances at Elena.

She nods at him. "You can tell him, Vic. He fixed Sylvia's TV. He's good."

Victor holds up the switch, pointing at it. "I create them at my emporium. It's a game piece. For the game. You know .. . a secret game."

"Every player has a switch," Elena adds. "It's part of the basic kit. A new round is starting soon."

The breath catches in my throat, and my mouth feels dry despite being soaked. "If a magical Fix-It-Switch is a game piece, what is the board?"

"The world," Victor says.

My mouth drops open. "And what's the objective?"

"To change it."

I stare at them both. "To change the world? How?"

Victor shrugs, as if it's an ordinary day. "There are rules and things. Those in the game, they know how." He stashes the switch in his pocket. "I will fix this at the emporium. Come, Elena. I'll get a cab." He heads towards the street and flags a taxi.

"Thank you for helping Sylvia," Elena says.

I manage to nod.

"Andrew, I can tell that today was a lot for you. So, if you want, you can go back home to your normal life and routine. That's okay."

Go back? I think of the four walls waiting at my apartment, and the thumbnail faces, and the open delivery box that brought me a Fix-It-Switch this morning, wondering if I can even *go* back to normal knowing such a thing exists.

Trisha's statement about me *hating change* pops in my head, and I'm locked in, wondering if that actually feels like me or if I just haven't come across a change that I want.

"But," she says with a smile, "if going back to normal life is not what you want today, there's probably room in that cab for you, too. *If* you're willing to squeeze in next to Victor." Elena turns and walks away.

I stand there—soaked, sore, bruised, exhausted, and Trisha is still gone. And, I realize, despite all that, nothing like what I was this morning before I opened the box.

There's something new.

"Wait!" I call after her. "I'm in."

11

INLAND

JENNIFER MONSEN

"What's with the lighthouse?"

Sandra glanced at her stepson in the rearview mirror; his reflection met her gaze with a scowl, then turned back to the window. He'd been the one to ask the question, but somehow Caspian always seemed angry the moment he noticed her looking at him.

"The lighthouse?" Sandra looked back at the road, which seemed to extend endlessly into the red rock of the desert.

Of course, she knew the lighthouse. She knew it better than her own home. But she hadn't expected Caspian to notice the old building, and she needed a moment to find the words to explain.

"The lighthouse. You know, tower with a big light on top? Usually found by the ocean? But for some reason there's one here?" Caspian turned his face back to the sandblasted structure that stood like a finger rising from the desert stone.

"Well, you see..." Sandra trailed off. How did she begin to

explain? Especially to a boy like Caspian, who always cringed and complained at every attempt she made to build their relationship?

But then, wasn't it a full moon tonight?

Sandra pulled over to the side of the road and rolled down her window. She closed her eyes and breathed in through her nose. She smelled only desert heat, at first. But there, so faint you might never notice, she caught it: the slightest hint of brine.

One of those nights. She couldn't miss this chance.

Sandra turned back in her seat to meet Caspian's scowl with a smile. "I could tell you," she said, "or I could show you."

———

"This wasn't always a desert," Sandra explained as they clanged their way up the rusty metal stairs of the lighthouse.

The hot air tasted like dust and neglect. Though the sun still cleared the horizon, the tower walls kept the staircase in a cavern-like darkness. Caspian used his phone as a flash-light, but Sandra didn't need her eyes to find the way.

"Thousands of years ago, this was all the bed of an inland sea." Sandra had seen the fossils: tight-spiraled shells and fish with many ribs embedded into stones on mountain peaks. "That's how you get places like the salt flats—and those ridges on the mountains? Paleolithic beach."

"Thanks for the history lesson." Even without looking, Sandra could hear the eyeroll in Caspian's voice. "But unless you're telling me dinosaurs built this, I don't see what it has to do with anything."

"Just setting the stage."

Sandra started to huff and puff. At Caspian's age, she could have taken all these stairs in a run. Was she so much older now? But, yes, now that she stopped to think, she hadn't come here in at least a decade. It was so far away, and life got busy, and all of a sudden, she had grey hair and aches and pains and a surly twelve-year-old stepson who now followed her like a reluctant shadow. She was surprised Caspian hadn't put up more of a fight about coming; he didn't usually care for any plan she suggested. But he must have been curious, like she once had been.

The glass at the top of the lighthouse had broken long ago, leaving the shattered remains of the lantern coated in a thin film of grit. Sandra picked her way across the familiar debris to stand at the guard rail.

"We'll have to wait a bit." Sandra pointed at the sun, only now touching the distant mountains with one edge.

"What about dinner?" Caspian whined.

"We'll eat later. It'll be worth it," Sandra promised.

"What will be worth it?"

When she didn't answer, Caspian dragged himself over to the guardrail with a groan. He leaned over the railing so far she almost grabbed him to keep him from falling over—but that would have gone about as well as trying to grab an angry bobcat.

"Wait. You'll see."

———

The shadow of the tower jutted out like a sundial, then faded into the spreading dusk. The air started to cool as the sun vanished little by little. They waited in silence, Caspian fidgeting, Sandra held still by the weight of memory.

"My grandfather was the last lighthouse keeper here," Sandra said as the dusk began to fade into true dark. "They stopped bothering once the town went from a boom town to a ghost town. So, there's no money to fix the lantern anymore. But I still like to visit from time to time."

"You said you were going to show me something." Caspian yawned. "So far all you've shown me is broken glass and a bunch of rocks. I should have stayed in the car—"

"Listen!" Sandra shushed him. "Can you hear it?"

"Hear what?" Caspian grumbled—but when the sound came again, she knew he'd heard it too.

"Thunder?" he asked.

"There's not a cloud in the sky," Sandra said, waving a hand at the expanse of stars above.

"Then...what is it?"

"The tide." Sandra smiled at Caspian, his face dimly lit by the moon. "I told you, this place used to be an inland sea. And sometimes, on nights like tonight, the sea comes back to visit the desert it used to call home."

The water burst from the surrounding mountains with a deafening roar. Waves slammed against the side of the tower, water drops sparkling like diamonds in the air as they caught the moonlight. Caspian might have gasped or cried out—for that matter, Sandra might have herself—but no sound they made would have pierced that massive roar. The shelter of the old lighthouse was the only thing that kept them from being swept away.

———

The flood lasted for what seemed like hours. Then the water settled and stilled into gentler waves, no longer deafening.

"So, worth leaving the car?" Sandra asked Caspian. He stared at her, wide eyed. "My brother and I used to take out a rowboat, see how far we could get before the ocean left again in the morning. That old thing is probably rotted away by now; too bad."

"I think there's something swimming out there," Caspian said, voice faint.

Sandra peered into the dark until she saw the gleam of a massive fin breaking through the surf. "Oh, yes. One of those ate my oar once. I can never remember what they're called..."

"It's... it's so big," Caspian said, and he could have meant the prehistoric fishes or the sea itself.

"Old, too," Sandra said, smiling at the familiar waves. "Older than whale song. The sea and the desert go a long way back."

"But...why did the sea go away, then?" Caspian asked. "If it's just going to come back?"

"I don't know," she admitted. "Why does the sea come back, if it's just going to go away again?"

"That's the same thing," Caspian said.

"If you say so." Sandra watched as the water began to recede. "Let's head down; it's shallow enough now we can wade back to the car. Your dad's going to be wondering what's taking us so long."

"Can we stay a little longer?" Caspian asked, and Sandra smiled.

"Sure," she said. "And we can always come back again." Sandra didn't dare touch him, not yet—but she stepped closer to Caspian, and for once he didn't pull away. They stood together for a long time, close as the sea and the desert, as the crash of waves on sandstone whispered an ancient song of home.

DOOR NUMBER TWO

VINCENT H. O'NEIL

When they want the job done messy, they give it to me. That usually means they're trying to send a message, but sometimes it just means the target ticked them off. Either way, it calls for a lot of blood and a body that's going to be found. You might think that causes me a lot of trouble, given the added degree of difficulty, but you'd be wrong. Although I get paid very well for the work I do, I'd honestly do it for free—and I'd do it the same way.

When I started out, it was because of a guy from the neighborhood named Mattins. He's connected to the Regents, who are the heads of a local organized crime outfit. Mattins had seen me fight in the streets many times, and when I was seventeen, he decided I was scrappy enough to earn a tryout. Mattins believes in an organized approach where you learn a lot about your targets, study their habits, and make it look like an accident. I tried to follow his advice at first, but it didn't work for me. I ended up doing it the hard way more often than not, up close in a frenzy because the target was spooked or running, and I discovered something that I hadn't expected.

I liked doing it that way. I'm good-sized and very strong, and in a pinch, I can always reach down and find what it takes to come out on top. It helps that I work out quite a bit. I spend a lot of time running the streets to build up my wind, because when one of my jobs is over, I have to get out of there fast. Like I said, I do it messy. And loud.

If that sounds stupid, it means you just don't know. There's a level of excitement in my method that is beyond description. As the years went by, I asked for less and less information about a target and found I liked it more and more. Going in blind like that gives me a rush that's just one notch short of a heart attack. The only thing that comes close to it is driving fast on a dark, empty road with your lights turned off. There's a giddy exhilaration that just takes you over, not knowing what's coming up next. And there's a mind-blowing power that comes from accepting the notion that you're going to have to deal with whatever pops up. You swerve around that abandoned car that just appeared out of nowhere, or you slam right into it.

————

I live my life in a simple way. No phones, no email, no credit cards. When I get an assignment, it's a scrap of paper handed to me by some street kid. The paper comes from Mattins, but he only meets me after the fact, to pay me in cash when the job is done.

My last job for the Regents came as a street address specifying that my next victim lived in Apartment B. I memorized it and destroyed the piece of paper. I then donned a rough set of clothes that I wouldn't mind burning later on and went to get my tools. For me, it's almost always a knife, spring-loaded and extremely sharp. A long trip on the subway and a short jaunt on a bus put me a mile away from the target, and I walked the rest. I always work late at night.

I already knew it was in a nasty part of town, but the place itself was even shabbier than I'd expected. It stood on a street lined with other two-stories, but even for this neighborhood, it was run down. The bottom floor was an abandoned shop, and the second floor couldn't have held more than two apartments. It was a cloudy no-moon night, so I was able to walk all the way around the building without overly exposing myself. During that little hike, I found the only entrance, a back door that led straight up an enclosed flight of stairs.

I also saw the mailboxes, which had no names on them. That was all fine until I noticed that the apartments were marked with numbers and not letters. Apartment One and Apartment Two, not Apartment A and Apartment B. It was well past midnight and no one was on the street, so I found a good shadow and pondered my next move.

I was sure the slip of paper had said Apartment B. I still am.

So what to do? Assume that Apartment Two was Apartment B? It made sense, but Mattins and the Regents don't like guesswork. They would not be pleased if I killed whoever was in Apartment Two when the target was in

Apartment One, so I made a quick decision. I was going to have to clear both sets of rooms. I studied the building's back wall from my hiding place, noticing a difference in the windows to the left and right. The stairs went up to a narrow hallway, so it was safe to assume the two apartments were to either side of that. The one on the right showed no light at all, but the one to the left was lit up despite the late hour. Abrupt flashes on the drapes suggested someone was watching television, and I hoped it was an insomniac who would give me a contest and not somebody who'd nodded off in an armchair.

That was everything I could determine by looking at the building.

My preference for minimal information may seem a little crazy at this point, but it's actually the best part about this work. No matter what I encounter, it all comes down to a willingness to do whatever it takes. Sometimes that means going after a victim who is unexpectedly alert, or even armed. Sometimes it means fighting more than one opponent. Sometimes it means chasing people down who are literally running for their lives. And sometimes it means killing everyone there, just to be sure.

This was obviously one of those just-to-be-sure times, and I felt the thrill rising. In the early days, I would experience that wild anticipation just observing a target, but over time, it had become muted. Now, only the truly risky assignments revived that adrenaline-laced rush—which is another reason why I'd stopped asking for specifics. I forced myself to stand there in the shadows, savoring the thump of my heart and the dryness of my mouth, until all I could think of was getting in there. Getting at whoever was in there.

I slipped across to the door and picked the lock with ease. Closing it silently, I went up the stairs with the lightest of steps. The hallway ended at a window that showed the streetlamps in front of the building, and a single overhead bulb in a filthy casing cast the corridor in dull orange. I heard the television now, and noted it was coming from Apartment Two. I smiled at the way its clamor would mask any sounds I might make while getting into Apartment One. I expected that the occupant(s) of the darkened unit would be asleep, and so I decided to clear that set of rooms before taking on the insomniac.

I had time and savored the thrill of those final moments. I inspected Apartment One's weak wooden door, and then gently pressed my fingertips against it. Nothing was securing it other than its antiquated lock, and no vibrations of any kind came from within. After you do enough of these jobs, you can almost sense the presence of life on the other side of the door, but this time nothing registered. Even so, I made sure the knife was where I could get it quickly and picked the lock.

Apartment One wasn't as dark inside as I'd expected, but that was because there were no drapes on the windows. I slid inside and closed the door, my ears questing for a snore or a bedspring or some indication of occupancy. There was nothing, so I let my eyes adjust to the semi-darkness. I was in the apartment's front room, and a doorway leading into the back was to my right. There was a musty smell to the place, and I began to wonder at the lack of furniture.

That wasn't proof positive that no one lived there; in a lousy dump like this one, lack of possessions is not uncommon. But the silence, and the overall sense that nothing living was inside these walls, suggested that the error in the address was going to make no difference. No one lived in Apartment One, so it didn't matter if Apartment Two was Apartment B or not. There was someone in *there* that I was being paid to kill, after I finished checking out Apartment One. The excitement returned as I quietly moved across the empty room to the doorway leading into the back.

I must confess that I was already plotting how to enter the insomniac's place when it all happened. I wasn't concentrating, but in the end, I doubt it would have made much difference. The doorway led into a bedroom with a single window on the building's back wall, and so the lighting in there wasn't quite as good. An open door probably led to a bathroom, but I never got to see if that was the case.

The bedroom was almost bare, but after a moment, I saw that a small shape was outlined against the window. At first, I thought it was a mop, standing on its handle with the head against the glass, but then it shifted slightly. And spoke.

"Hello there." The two words were in the voice of a very young girl, friendly and welcoming.

The mop resolved into shoulder-length hair, and then she appeared to stand up. Seeing her silhouetted against the glass, I suddenly realized she was too tall for a child. My hand was already reaching for the knife when she launched at me.

"Let's play." The voice was now a young woman's, and she came on like an attack dog.

The distance wasn't great, but she covered it just as my blade was snapping open. Maybe the shadows played a trick on me, but I swear she zigzagged impossibly as she crossed the floor. I couldn't get a clear view of her blurred form, but my instincts are good, and so is my timing. I ducked my shoulder, twisted my hand so that she'd impale herself on the point of the knife, and braced for the impact.

It never came. Nothing slammed into the knife, and the only sign that she'd come close to me was a brush of wet hair that slipped across my cheek like a tiny breeze. Without understanding it, I knew she was behind me, and so I bent my knees to dive away. That was when a claw-like hand gripped my left shoulder and a blade rasped against the inside of my crotch.

I've been cut before, but had never experienced anything like that. The blade came up right where the inside of my left leg ended and grated against the bone after it parted the cloth and the flesh. Even now, if I shut my eyes, I can still feel that nauseating scrape and the way it ran all the way up into my brain. I screamed so hard that my voice broke, sounding just like so many of my victims over the years.

When you get cut like that, your entire existence shrinks to that spot. I dropped my knife, grabbed my groin with both hands, and collapsed on the floor in a ball. Every one of my muscles constricted in an effort to put pressure on the gash. Blood ran over my fingers as I tried to locate the wound and squeeze it shut, praying that she hadn't hit the artery. She hadn't, but at the time I couldn't tell.

The girl could have easily finished me off, and I was so focused on stanching the blood that I completely forgot her until she opened the door and left. I looked up for just a second, but again she was a blur. The door across the hall opened from the inside, and she passed into the light as if she lived there. The door shut, and I went back to clutching the slick flesh and the hot liquid and hoping for the first time in my life that someone was calling the cops.

———

Somebody did call them, and it was the guy behind Door Number Two. I only know that because it was what the cops said when I awoke from surgery many hours later. I had already passed out when the "little old man" across the hall left his apartment and walked out of the building never to return, so I didn't hear him—or the girl—making their exit. It was nice of him to call for help before bugging out, but it was also very weird.

The police seemed to think so, anyway. I pretended to be muddled by the anesthetic, so they delayed the questioning until I'd had enough time to come up with a flimsy story. I said I'd been lured into the empty apartment by a young woman who had then stabbed and robbed me. There was plenty of blood on my fallen knife by the time they got there, but apparently, my wound didn't match the blade. The doctors said that the only time they'd seen a cut like mine had been a tiger attack at the zoo, but the cops decided to ignore that.

They ignored all the other holes in my story, too, and I soon realized they were uneasy about this case and wanted it to go away. They told me the little old man in Apartment

Two had rented the place using a false name and that no one knew much about him. He hadn't been there long, and he'd disappeared without a trace. They asked one bizarre question about whether or not I'd ever studied archeology and clammed up once I said no. I tried to get them to explain where that question had come from, but they'd received the answer they wanted and ended the investigation.

I met with Mattins three weeks later, once he was sure I wasn't being watched. Using a cane, I hobbled to a park near my place. We sat back to-back on a set of benches in a secluded spot, and he didn't waste any time with formalities.

"You're not getting paid, in case you were wondering."

"I wasn't."

"Some people are very unhappy with you."

"Some people should have given me the right address."

He shifted his big frame to give me a critical look. "You got the right address. You went in the wrong room."

"I was being thorough."

"Thorough? That other apartment was empty. Hadn't been rented in months."

"It wasn't empty."

Mattins gave an ugly laugh. "So, you surprised some homeless old lady, and she almost killed you. More reason not to go in the wrong room."

"Cops said the target was an old man. He called them before he ran off."

"We know who the target was. You would have known too, if you weren't so crazy."

"He called for help. For *me*. And that homeless old lady you mentioned? She moved like an Olympic gymnast. She went across the hall after putting me down, and he let her in."

"Nonsense."

"I saw it."

"You were bleeding out. Who knows what you saw?"

It was my turn to be critical. "What aren't you telling me? What are you hiding?"

"Not a thing. The target owed the Regents money, and you were supposed to make an example out of him. You screwed it up."

"Cops asked if I was into archeology. That ring any bells?"

"No."

"If you're not going to tell me anything, why are we talking?"

"I am telling you something. You're fired, because the cops know you now. You were a phantom before this, and that was the only thing keeping you on the payroll. The Regents were creeped out by your methods, but you'd always delivered. Now you've failed in a big way, and so you're out." He stood, looking down at me. "It was just a matter of time, doing things the way you did them. I was always dreading the day when one of your jobs would end with you caught or killed. But this, this *disaster* you created, is so crazy and so stupid that I don't feel bad at all. Goodbye."

He started walking away, but I'd come with a request. "Mattins?"

"Don't ask for money."

"I'm not. I'm asking for something I never wanted before. Send a kid around with the old man's name."

"No. He's long gone, and you'll be out of action for months."

"That girl was with him. He's the only way I'm going to find her."

"You really are insane, aren't you?" The big man gave me a look that bordered on pity. "After what she did to you, you still want to go after her?"

"Look at it this way: If I find them, I can finish the job. And it'll be free."

He shook his head, an exhausted parent giving up on a willful child.

"You're out. Be happy they aren't handing someone *your* address."

———

It took me months to recover, but I stayed busy. Very little was known about the old man and his female companion, except for street rumors. The most common story said he was a foreigner who had tried to fence a rare artifact through the Regents. The man was supposed to be a famous archeologist, and the item was alleged to have been stolen from a dig in the Middle East. At first eager to do the deal, the Regents had backed off suddenly—and quickly. I entered the picture soon after that, and it cost me my best client.

My special set of skills is always in demand, however, so I went back to work as soon as I was able. I tested myself one night by going for a walk in the park, leaning heavily on the cane even though I hadn't needed it in weeks. Two helpful young men tried to mug me, so I stabbed one in the throat and hunted the other one down. I've had several jobs since then, for different clients, but the thrill just isn't there anymore.

I know where it is. It's back in that empty apartment, but not in the way you think. I'm not the least bit scared. The girl's talents had ended the encounter quickly, but they lived on in my mind. None of my targets ever offered anywhere near the challenge she did, and I felt cheated. The fact that she didn't bother to finish me off was salt in the wound, and so I kept digging for any sign of where they might have gone. Nothing solid turned up, and so I'd slowly begun to accept that I might not ever come to grips with her again.

That all changed this morning, however, when a street kid handed me a scrap of paper. An address was written on it, with four words: *They're back. Are you?*

It's been a tough day since then, as I've had to force myself to stay put until nightfall. I decided to write this all down in the hopes that it would help make the time go by. I've been riding a euphoric rollercoaster for hours, anticipating the night's activities, and at times I simply can't sit still.

I have no idea how this will turn out. I have no idea why they came back. I have no idea how the Regents found them. I have no idea why that girl was inside that unrented apartment. I have no idea what she can really do. Or even what she is.

And that, my friends, is the biggest thrill of all.

WHEN THE HILLS BREATHE
MCKEL JENSEN

"The hills are breathing today," Granddad said from the table, pointing outside our house.

I hurried to the window. The hills, always soft and rolling beneath their grassy cloak, now undulated slowly, as if giants breathed beneath them.

"Do you want to go play?" Father asked.

I looked at my sister, her braid down her back. The two of us ran toward the green mounds, hearing my dad and granddad laughing sweetly. Our feet were unsteady on the grass as it shifted, but the ground gave us a soft landing each time we fell. At first, we held hands—uncertain on our feet— but soon realized we needed both hands to balance.

I had heard of this before. Dad spoke of it—so did Mom before she left. The hills don't breathe as often as they used to, but we were there to witness it now, to roll with it, to see the beautiful breath as life came back to our land.

"Look at Daisy," Racheal said. The dog barked and hesitantly put a foot forward. Soon, she was rolling as if it were her own form of catnip.

The three of us scampered and tumbled from one rise to another, cascading down when the inhales were big and running up when there was an exhale. We made it to the top of the biggest one and collapsed, spread-eagle in the grass, breathing as deeply as the ground beneath us.

"I can almost reach the clouds," I said, "and then I'm pulled away." We laughed as our hands reached up as if believing it made it possible.

"Almost got it!" Racheal said in defeat before we both laughed again.

"Ugh," I said as the clouds moved further away. "I give up."

Out of breath, I looked at Daisy, resting comfortably on her belly with her head on her front legs. I scratched behind her ear and snuggled in to hold her.

It was uncertain how long the land would be like this. As the sun moved below the horizon and the hills' breath began to deepen into a slumber, Racheal and I (followed by Daisy) started home, watching each step as the earth continued to undulate beneath us.

"Do we have school tomorrow?" Racheal asked as we entered our home.

"No, sweet girl," Father said. "The hills are breathing. We will stay home."

Racheal and I grinned.

"Does this happen where Grandma was from? Or where cousin Arthur goes in the summer? I've never heard anyone outside our village talk about the hills," I said.

"No," Granddad said. "Our hills speak only to us, just as the trees in our forest watch over only us."

Racheal and I sat down at the table to eat; the others had already finished.

"What did the hills have to say to you?" Granddad asked me.

It hadn't occurred to me to listen. If our land's trees wake to watch over my family with their eyes, why couldn't breathing hills speak?

"What do they say to you, Granddad?" I asked.

Granddad smiled and leaned in closer. "They said," he paused to rub my head, "that it's time to teach you how to listen."

That evening as the house settled into the routine of bedtime activities, I sat in our field beneath a tree facing the hills. They still moved up and down in their gentle, rhythmic pattern.

"Tree," I said. "What do you see? What do the hills have to say?"

My hand fell to the grass near a family of roly-polies climbing over each other. One bug was upside down away from the group, trying to roll itself back over.

"I've got you, little guy," I said, extending a finger for it to latch onto.

I watched as it climbed over my hand and fingers before rolling into a ball. I placed it back with its family and waited for it to unravel, but it didn't. The rest of the family moved off and congregated again further away before my bug friend finally uncoiled and rolled onto his back. Each time I attempted to push him over onto his feet, he curled back up in a ball.

The sun set, and I felt the tree close its eyes.

That night, I had a dream of a man that looked like my father. Thin. Tall. Dark hair. But this man had glasses and a funny mustache. His body was stiff, not like a corpse, but rather he wasn't able to bend his arms or legs. And when he turned to look behind him, his whole body moved with him.

"Granddad," I asked at breakfast. "Who was the man in my dream?"

Grandad sipped his coffee. "Is that what the hills were telling you?"

I shrugged. How was I supposed to know? I didn't know the language of the hills.

"Go out again today when the hills are awake and listen," he said.

Disappointment settled in my chest as I wanted Granddad to tell me, but my heart told me he wouldn't.

"Racheal, want to come back to the breathing hills with me?" I asked, but Racheal was busy playing with her doll, so I ventured out alone.

I passed the trees, planted my feet in the ground before the breathing hills, and asked them, "What is it you want to teach me?"

My lungs filled deep with air, and I exhaled. I soon found my breath in rhythm with the hills and stepped onto them, rocking at first, but by matching the rhythm of the land, I never stumbled.

On top of the big hill where Racheal and I sat the day

before. I lay down looking at the sky. I whispered, "I'm listening."

The clouds danced. A woman in a dress twirled across the sky. She was soon joined by a man. Arm in arm, the two waltzed and glided, sweeping the sky with their joy in imperfect harmony. At the end of their dance, the man twirled the woman to the other side of the sky, and when she turned back to the man, she revealed a baby nestled in her arms. She looked up to her partner on the other end of the horizon and extended her arms, presenting the baby to him. The man stood stiff and took a step back before running off, out of sight.

My heart hurt for the woman as the clouds around her darkened and began to weep. She shielded the baby from the storm until sunbeams broke through the clouds one by one. And as the child grew, more and more sunbeams came, and the girl began to dance with her mother. When the girl reached the height of the mother, the mother stopped the playful twirling, clutched her chest, and collapsed to the ground. The girl raced to her mother and embraced her, and storm clouds swirled.

Eventually, the dark clouds parted and I could see the girl, head down, mourning at the place where her mother was laid. Alone, the girl, now a woman, made her way through the dark as the clouds lifted gradually. A man walked into the scene and she shook her finger at him. She had known her mother was hurt by a man, and she wasn't about to repeat the past. She dismissed a line of suitors, one by one–each charming in their own way. But one sat beside her and made her smile. And he asked her to dance.

The clouds lightened, and just like the generation before, the two swept the sky clean. And just like the generation before, the woman turned to reveal a baby, and she held it out to the man across the way.

That's me, I thought.

I watched with anticipation to see if the generational story would repeat itself, but I already knew the outcome of the story. As expected, Father ran to her and held the little bundle and stayed.

"Granddad," I said, running back to the house. "Granddad, the sky danced for me. I saw my mom." Sadness weaved through my excitement.

"Oh!" Granddad said, reaching out for me to sit with him.

I did, and he listened closely as I told what I had seen.

"That is incredible," he said. "The sky had a lot to show you."

"It did," I said.

"What did the sky teach you?" Granddad asked.

"Granddad," I said with caution, "I told you what it taught me."

Granddad paused. "You told me what you saw," he said. "But what did you learn?"

It took me a minute to form the words. "Grandad, I am loved," I said.

"Yes, you are," he said. "But you already knew that."

I nodded, feeling a warm glow swell in my chest.

After a moment, Granddad said, "You've told me a beautiful story. You know you are loved. The sky danced for you. But what did the hills tell you?"

The question lingered over me through the evening and

into the early morning. The question guided my legs to leave the house as the sun was rubbing sleep from the sky. The air felt crisp through my pajamas, but I was refreshed with new hope.

Again, I found rhythm in the hills and climbed to the highest spot. The line of light marked the time across the countryside. From this spot, I watched the river stream through the land, the distant mountains greeting the morning, and the insects hovering over the grass around me.

"Hills," I sighed. "What do you have to teach me?"

In the valley below, a fox pounced on a mouse. The fox took the freshly caught food back to the den where a small litter eagerly waited.

I wondered where the mother fox roamed and why the male fox watched over the brood. And then I saw her walking in the distance in a patch of wild flowers. I watched her lie down, die, and decompose as the grass grew through her and new flowers grew strong in her place.

I saw the cubs leave their home and play, tugging on each other. They rolled in the grass and played throughout the patch of wild flowers as they grew.

Did they know their mother fed those flowers?

The wild flower patch grew as I witnessed generations of foxes occupying the area, dying and feeding new growth, and the land continued to live.

The hills began to slow, and I wiped my face with my hand. I planted my hand firmly on the ground beneath me and thanked the hills for their gift. The grass intertwined snugly in my fingers before gently letting go.

Granddad was waiting at the back door for me, and I greeted him with a hug.

He kissed my head and said, "What did they tell you, child?"

I smiled up at the hills and saw them take a deep breath. "Our family is part of the land," I said.

Through the back window, I saw Father and Racheal settling in for breakfast around the table.

"I love you, Granddad."

"Oh, child," he said, hugging me again. "Our family's stories are preserved here, and it always has such wonderful stories to tell, if we listen."

MEMORIES THAT NEVER WERE
IKECHUKWU HENRY

"Dear Uche m."

The voice always got him whenever he played the video. Was it the way his name was pronounced, *'Who-che,'* as though tasting it for the first time? Or was it the soothing depth of the speaker's tone, the familiarity of this stranger he knew nothing about? The melanin-skinned man in the video blended seamlessly with the deepening evening sky behind him, as though heaven was about to release a heavy cry upon the earth. Yet, despite how vivid the background seemed, Uche couldn't place it. He couldn't recognize the setting where the video was recorded, nor could he pick out anything remotely familiar.

And so, he stopped trying.

He let his gaze roam over his art studio—the only place where his mind found clarity, where colors, shapes, and emotions merged to create meaning. His private sanctuary wasn't just a room; it was a testament to the art that had consumed, shaped, and refined his soul for as long as he could remember. The walls were lined with wooden boards, pinned sketches, and canvases of different sizes, some half-finished, some abandoned. Paintings leaned against one another in a disordered pile, like old, forgotten memories waiting to be revived.

With a sigh, Uche played the video once more.

"I shouldn't be doing this, honestly," the man in the video admitted, his voice carrying a quiet sadness. *"I should have allowed nature to run its course. But I thought...why not leave a memory of me—of us—for you to cling to? Even if you don't remember any of this happening."*

Uche exhaled sharply and pushed aside his charcoal pencil, his paintbrush stiff with dried acrylic, and scattered sheets of unfinished work. He made space for the painting he had been working on for months—the very place the man in the video spoke about. A place Uche couldn't recall yet felt compelled to recreate.

His brows furrowed as he listened.

"The first time I saw you, you were wearing a tailored Ankara dress with a designer bag."

Uche almost laughed. A dress? He shook his head, dismissing it as a translation issue—perhaps the man meant a shirt with Ankara prints.

"I could tell you were in a hurry, ordering coffee at Kaleb Coffee Shop, which was always brimming with people every morning. I was always there, you know—sitting in the same spot, watching early risers rush to work, some heading to the market, carrying their goods in modernized vehicles."

The man chuckled, and Uche found himself smiling. He

didn't know what was more amusing, the stranger's laughter or the stunned curiosity in his voice at seeing traders using vehicles to transport goods. Here, in his own reality, traders still carried their loads on their heads, trekking long distances because the government had refused to refine the infrastructure, sending the economy into a downward spiral.

"But what struck me wasn't your haste, nor your outfit, but what you carried. Can you guess?"

Uche already knew. He had played the video too many times.

"It was a painting. A fountain. Two young men watching the water rise and fall. It was magical, that painting. I felt an undeniable pull to approach you. But you were already hurrying out, and I was left with a sour taste of regret for not manning up and stopping you."

The man's voice dimmed slightly, as if weighed down by the memory, his sadness slipping between words like a current passing through water.

"I was heartbroken by your departure..."

The sadness didn't last long. The tone shifted—lighter, unmasking an excitement that made Uche's pulse quicken.

"I wish you could feel what I felt when I saw you walk in again another day."

The video clip shifted, revealing more of the background. The softly lit interior. Sleek yet homely. A coffee shop, but unlike anything Uche had ever seen. It was modern, yet ethereal. The walls held murals, fluid, shifting in colors that seemed almost alive, something out of a sci-fi movie. Not something that existed here, in his world. A chandelier hung above the man, its intricate design casting an ambient glow over plush, velvety seats. The counter—polished black marble—reflected warm lighting, and behind it, golden coffee machines gleamed like relics from a future untouched by time.

And then, the name struck him.

Kaleb Coffee Shop.

Uche had found himself googling it, scouring the internet for any mention of its location. But there was nothing. No website. No records. As if it had never existed.

As if it were merely a scene from a forgotten dream.

Determined, he had ventured out with a copy of his unfinished painting tucked under his arm. He had searched the city, visited the closest coffee shop he could find—miles away—hoping to recognize something, anything. He had stood at the street corner where the shop should have been, according to the man's description.

But there was no coffee shop. Instead, a towering mansion loomed where the café was meant to be.

When he asked the locals, they regarded him strangely, claiming no such place had ever existed in their neighborhood. It left him embarrassed. Frustrated. Maybe even a little mad at himself.

Yet, as he walked away from that spot, he couldn't shake the feeling that something was off.

Like the shop had been there once.

Just... not in this reality.

And that thought terrified him.

But even more terrifying was the question that followed—

Who was this man in the video, and why did Uche feel like he should have known him?

"But this time, I approached you."

The man's voice was steady, laced with a quiet certainty that sent a shiver through Uche's spine.

"You were nice and welcoming—far more than I had expected. You told me your name was Uchenna, twenty-five years old, and an artist." A chuckle escaped the man's lips, but there was something wistful in the sound. *"You giggled shyly when you said you were an artist, and I could hear the embarrassment in your voice. Why were you shy to name your passion? Your profession? I wanted to ask, but before I could, you told me you were a medical student— that painting was just a side hustle, something you did in your free time. And I felt bad, Uche. Bad that you diminished your own artistry as if you didn't recognize the power that lived at the tip of your brush."*

Uche clenched his jaw. There it was again. This man knew too much about him, spoke of him with an intimacy that unnerved him. Yet, Uche knew nothing in return. Not even the man's name. Not once had he uttered it.

"We exchanged numbers, called often. We chatted on Whats-App. Every moment we spent together was never boring. You talked about your art, the process, the things you longed to paint. Once, you told me that if you could paint a feeling, it would be this moment—" There was a brief pause, and then the man's voice softened.

"—The quiet hum of the coffee shop after everyone had left. The warmth of my hand over yours. The glow of the city outside."

Uche exhaled sharply. It was like hearing a story about a stranger who happened to share his name, his passion. It wasn't possible. And yet, everything about it felt disturbingly real—a flicker of something deep and buried, just out of reach, like a dream that had slipped through the cracks of his memory.

"We met often, always at our table by the window. You used to say the street looked different from here—softer somehow, like a painting in motion. Sometimes we wouldn't even talk. You would just sketch on the rough paper you always carried, and I would watch you."

Uche's brush glided over the canvas, painting a large window, its glass slightly fogged, the blurred city lights beyond it. The man's words guided his hand, as though they had been buried somewhere deep within him all along.

"And you loved the lights at night," the man continued. "The way they cast ethereal pools on the streets, especially during special festivals like Easter and Valentine's. So, we decided to recreate it." The man's eyes softened on the screen, as though on the verge of revealing an unimaginable secret.

"The first time you kissed me and told me you loved me, it was right here, at this table. You told me that some moments shouldn't be cleaned away. That imperfections sometimes make things more beautiful." A soft, knowing smile curled the man's lips, the kind that carried warmth and old familiarity, like he knew what his words were doing to Uche, how they unraveled something inside him.

"Uche m," the man whispered, his voice tinged with nostalgia, smooth yet fragile. *"I know you don't remember, but we used to sit here, by the window, where the lights made your skin glisten. You loved the paintings at the entrance, said they inspired one of your unfinished works. You even painted here, once.*

You wanted to capture how time felt in this place—how it stretched and folded over itself. How we could exist in two realities at once...forever and nowhere at all."

Uche's fingers tightened around his brush. He turned his gaze back to the canvas, pausing the video. The coffee shop was beginning to take shape under his brushstrokes, built from the man's words, his descriptions—brought to life from the fragments in the video. Each stroke was deliberate, an attempt to recreate a place that might not exist.

His art studio was quiet, save for the rhythmic whisper of bristles against canvas. The windows let in slanted rays of afternoon sunlight, casting long, golden beams across the floor. Little shelves lined the walls, crammed with sketchbooks, tubes of paint, and unfinished drawings. But the space felt...small. *Incomplete.*

Something was missing.

Uche pressed play again.

The man tilted his head slightly, his gaze filled with something Uche couldn't name, yet could feel seeping through the screen—through his words, through the spaces between them.

And then, his voice trembled.

"One time, during the rainy season, the rain caught us midway through our time together. You told me you hated rainy days."

The man chuckled softly.

"But that day, you complained about the cold, so I wrapped my scarf around you. I know you won't remember."

Uche's breath hitched. His entire body went still.

No one except his family knew how much he despised

the cold, how easily he caught chills. His mother had always fussed over him, wrapping him in layers before he stepped outside during the rainy season.

"You pretended to hate the scarf, grumbling about how it smelled like me." The man smiled wistfully. "But when you thought I wasn't looking, you would bury your nose in it. I never told you. But I always noticed."

Uche's fingers trembled. His pulse thrummed in his ears. He was gripping the brush too tightly, his knuckles white against the handle.

Had this ever been real?

The coffee shop was slowly transforming on his canvas—the soft glow of its lights, the velvet seats, the warm, golden ambiance. Every detail poured out of him like an unspoken memory clawing its way back to the surface. Uche had never been to this place. And yet, as he layered color upon color, shadows upon light, he felt an ache settle deep in his chest.

An ache for something he couldn't name.

For something he had lost.

For something that should never have been forgotten.

His art had always been visceral, drawn from places within him that words could never reach. But now, for the first time, he wondered—

Had he just painted a memory?

Or was he losing his mind?

"You told me about your dream—your desire to paint something timeless, something that would etch your name into history."

The man's voice was steady, yet there was a quiet urgency beneath it.

"But you had no idea what to paint. You said you were partici-

pating in the biggest art residency of your career, but the deadline was closing in. And I know, Uche... I know you're running out of time."

Uche's breath hitched.

How did this man know about the residency? The very one he had been hoping to enter, the one barely a month away? How did he know that despite his best efforts, he still had no idea what to submit? That, in secret, he had considered finishing the coffee shop painting for his entry, if only he could bring himself to complete it?

But deep down, Uche never truly believed he could. He had been painting this same piece for a year now—ever since he had woken from the coma and seen this same video, sent by this same man, a stranger whose face he had never seen in real life. At first, he had tried to rationalize it. He had gone to the hospital, checked for anemia, checked for signs of dementia. But each test came back the same: medically, he was fine.

So why did nothing feel fine?

"I decided to make this video, here in our favorite place, to talk about us. And I hope it will be enough to inspire you, Uche."

The man's voice wavered slightly.

"I'm sorry. I shouldn't be doing this...but I had to."

Uche's paintbrush slipped from his fingers.

The video was about to time out.

A strange warmth pressed against his skin, like the ghost of something familiar, something lost. And for the briefest moment, he swore he smelled caramel and coffee. Or maybe it was just the scent of paint lingering in the air. But at the edge of his vision, something flickered—not much, just a glimmer, a ripple, like a memory trying to slot itself back into place.

Maybe this coffee shop had never existed in this timeline.

But somewhere, somehow—*it had.* And Uche wasn't ready to let it slip away.

This wasn't just a story. It was an erased memory, a recounting of something real, something stolen from him.

He had to find out why.

He had to know if it was possible for a spirit to exist across timelines, for a soul to have lived another life in a different reality. He had to ask his only living family—his mother—just how long he had been in a coma after the accident, the hit-and-run driver that knocked him into blackness on that day he was returning from lecture months ago. And he had to find out if a video could be sent across dimensions, if such a thing was even possible.

But first... He had to submit this painting.

Almost complete now, the imperfect strokes bled into one another, forming something raw, something hauntingly familiar.

Maybe imperfections did make things more human.

LUCKY SEVEN

SHAWN POLLOCK

The following is an excerpt from *Untold Vietnam: Mysterious and Unexplainable Accounts from the Vietnam War.*

First Class Petty Officer Carl Abrams, USN

In 1967, I was captain of a Patrol Boat, Riverine, or PBR, deployed in IV Corps, operating out of Đồng Tâm Base Camp in the Mekong Delta. My crew consisted of gunner's mate Burt Stock, engineman Jake Sukeforth, and seaman Walt Dineen. Officially, we were PBR 107, but we called our boat Lucky Seven, although our luck nearly ran out one hot night in May.

Our job consisted mainly of patrolling the delta. A lot of stop and search, looking for Viet Cong running weapons in their sampans, and naturally, that led to a few shooting matches. PBRs operated in pairs for just that reason. Lucky Seven partnered with PBR 288, captained by Jerry Jackson. If one crew stopped to inspect a suspicious vessel, the other crew stayed nearby for backup.

One night back at the base, I watched as a SEAL fire team, bristling with weaponry, boarded 288. The "men with green faces," as the VC called them, conducted their operations deep in the mangrove forests, and it fell to a PBR to take them to the jumping-off point. It looked like 288 had pulled the short straw that night.

I hated insertions. That meant long night trips upriver, navigating with as little light as we could. Then once the SEALs disembarked, we had to travel back alone.

Jackson, however, looked excited. He stood alongside the SEALs, his blond crewcut sharp, muscles tight under his shirt. I always thought he liked hot situations a little too much, wanted a search to turn into a battle. Sometimes while my guys were digging through smelly fishing nets in some peasant sampan, hoping we hadn't bought ourselves any explosive trouble, Jackson would fire a .50-caliber burst from 288's bow and make us and the Vietnamese jump out of our skins. We'd yell at him to knock it off, and he'd laugh and say, "Just showing them who's boss."

I knew he couldn't tell me where he was taking the SEALs that night, so instead I asked, "When you coming back?"

"I don't know. We might stay to watch the fireworks."

"Negative," I said. "Get back here as soon as you drop those guys. I don't want to patrol alone tomorrow." As reckless as Jackson could be, we still needed him in case things went south.

He gave me a lantern-jawed grin as he boarded his boat. Then 288 motored off across the inky river and into the mangroves.

I couldn't relax that night. The delta was never quiet, but even noises and movement I thought I'd gotten used to had me tossing in my bunk until dawn.

I kept an eye upstream the next morning, but 288 never showed. I stewed for a while, thinking Jackson really was hanging back, hoping to see a firefight. And we did indeed patrol alone that day.

But we only heard static every time we tried to raise them on the radio. And just before nightfall, Captain Freeman called us into the base and told us no one else had been able to contact 288 either. He unfolded a map and said, "Their objective was a village called Trồng Cây, at the mouth of this canal here."

I whistled in surprise. Trồng Cây was deeper in the delta than I'd ever taken Lucky Seven, surely deeper than Jackson had ever gone.

"Our intelligence indicates a major Viet Cong force will be coming down the canal in the next few days," Freeman continued. "288 inserted Fire Team Alpha—SEAL Team Two, half a klick above the village so they could intercept that force on its flank. Jackson reported that Team Two made a successful insertion at 0500, so we know they made it to the village and that the radio was functioning then. We want you to go to Trồng Cây tomorrow morning to find out if anyone saw 288 and pick up any other intelligence you can."

I didn't like the thought of going alone into a combat situation, but orders were orders, and we made ready to head out after another mostly sleepless night. None of us spoke Vietnamese, so Freeman assigned us a guide from the Army of the Republic of South Vietnam named Phan Bình. I'd seen him around the base, a skinny, smiley guy. When he stepped aboard Lucky Seven and found out where we were headed, that smile disappeared.

Stock piloted while Sukey and I tracked our progress on the map. Dineen manned the .50-caliber machine guns. Phan sat aft, his back against the rail, with an M-16 in his lap. I asked him if he knew anything about Trồng Cây, but he shook his head in a tight-lipped way, like he was seasick and trying to hold it down.

I started to feel a little weird myself, the further we went. The breeze died and a stuffy, moldy smell rose from the river. So did the heat. The mangrove forest grew thicker and higher, and Stock had to throttle back. The river became so tight in some places, the trees brushed both sides of the boat at the same time. Pretty soon, it felt like we were stuck inside a green, clammy hand squeezing tighter and tighter.

After a few hours of travel, we rounded a bend and the forest opened into a clearing. We had arrived in Trồng Cây.

Most of the villages I'd seen in the Mekong amounted to little more than shanty towns on stilts. Trồng Cây didn't look like it had been built at all, but rather like it had sprung from the same ancient soil that fed the trees and vines lining the river. Shaggy thatched roofs crouched dimly within green foliage that rose so high, the light filtering through became hazy and ethereal. Vietnamese peasants in black outfits and conical hats drifted among the trees like ghosts. Pigs squealed and chickens clucked, and the smell of smoke and fermented fish rolled over the water. I wondered how many Westerners had ever seen this place.

We spotted the mouth of the canal where it emptied into

the river and headed there. As we drew near, I noticed four girls. One sat on the bank, soaking her feet, but the other three sat in the river up to their waists. Black hair hung over their shoulders and down their backs, so long it disappeared into the water. They looked up when Lucky Seven came rumbling in. The one on the bank stood and took off for the village, but the other three ducked into the river itself.

Phan yelled something at the running girl. I don't know if it was what he said or the M-16 in his hand, but she stopped and shouted back. Phan yelled again, and she said something that sounded like "Me nyan noo."

Phan looked at the water where the three girls had disappeared. He mumbled something else, more to himself this time, as the girl dashed into the trees.

"What'd she say?" I asked, looking up and down the river. Those girls hadn't come up anywhere I could see. "Did you ask about Jackson?"

Phan shook his head. "She say, go away this place."

"What about those other three? Where did they go?"

"I don't know," Phan said. He grabbed my sleeve. "We go. This bad place."

I heard the pleading in his voice, but I couldn't leave without answers. "We need to find 288," I said. I sent Phan and Stock ashore to ask around the village. I would have gone myself, but those three girls had me worried about sabotage, and I wanted to stay with my boat.

I was still scanning the river a couple of hours later when Stock waved from the bank. We wheeled around and picked up him and Phan.

"Anything?" I asked.

"No one claims to have seen 288 or Jackson," Stock said.

Phan shook his head. "No 288. We go now."

I checked my watch. Nearly 1800 hours. I didn't like the idea of going back in the dark, plus we hadn't yet discovered what happened to Jackson and his crew. I refused to believe no one had noticed something that stuck out as badly as a PBR in this ancient setting. "We'll put in here overnight, then take another crack at it in the morning. Someone's got to know something."

Phan didn't argue with that, but he looked like I'd kicked him in the stomach. He went aft again, wouldn't talk, wouldn't eat the C-rations we broke out or the Oreos Dineen passed around. Just sat there with his rifle in his lap.

Since Stock and Phan had done the legwork in the village, I divided the overnight watches among the rest of us. Dineen took 2000 hours to midnight, at which time I relieved him.

I'd never experienced darkness like I did that night on the river next to Trông Cây, darkness so total it pressed against my eyeballs. No light came from the village, and the few stars visible through the forest canopy couldn't penetrate the gloom.

I had just started a letter home by my flashlight when I heard splashing in the river. Night in Vietnam is full of noises, but this splashing had a deliberate quality that put me on alert. I checked my watch and noted the time, 0205 hours. I swept the light across the river, leaning over the boat's rail, until I came to three round objects in the black water.

They glided toward Lucky Seven, barely making a ripple.

Dark except for three pairs of unblinking eyes showing just above the water.

They stopped six feet from the boat and rose high enough out of the river to reveal small noses, wide mouths, and pointed chins. White skin, not Caucasian but more like the belly of a fish. Black hair floated around them like river grass.

These were female faces, and I thought again of the three girls who had gone into the water. But that had been hours ago. This couldn't be the same trio, but then who was approaching my boat? I only knew I didn't want them near Lucky Seven.

I reached for my Colt 1911, but before I could issue a warning, something strange came over me. Those eyes held me in place, lulling my body and mind, like the vibrating engines in a battleship when you're deep in the hull.

The one in the middle spoke. "Do you bring harm?"

Her voice rang like a bell over the water, clear and oddly pleasant, and I thought for sure the rest of the crew would come. No one stirred.

I tried to answer, but my mouth had suddenly gone dry. I swallowed and tried again. "No harm. I'm looking for another boat like mine. Have you seen it?"

"Yes."

"What about the crew?"

"They brought harm."

Harm? I thought of Jackson's itchy trigger finger on the .50-caliber guns, of his desire to "watch the fireworks." What had he done here?

"Where are they?" I asked.

Rather than answer, the girl smiled. The river that had been so dark suddenly filled with a luminous yellow light, and I could see all the way to the riverbed, clear as drinking water.

I saw Lucky Seven's hull extending beneath the surface. I saw rocks and fish. And I saw these girls weren't treading water with human legs, but with long, scaly, finned tails that extended from their waists and writhed in a slow, twining pattern.

They weren't alone in the river, either. Other half-fish people skimmed along the riverbed, some upstream, some down.

That strange light also revealed the river's cavernous depth, much more than I thought possible. A familiar shape shimmered far below. I guessed it was at least fifty feet, but even through all that water, I could still make out the PBR with "288" emblazoned on the side, resting in the silt of the riverbed.

Four of the fish people swirled around 288. Their tails shook harder than the others, as though they were not used to them. One of them looked up at me. Dog tags on a chain around his neck whipped in the undercurrent. One muscular arm extended toward me. And eyes in a lantern-jawed face bored deep into mine.

I should have jumped back in shock. I should have screamed. Instead, I stared in fascination.

"Do you want to join us?" the girl asked.

I realized I did. Her voice, her eyes filled me with warmth and a promise of someplace safe. No Mekong Delta, no war, no stop-and-search shootouts or SEAL insertions. I felt as secure as if I were sitting in my living room at home. The light in the water dimmed and died, leaving us in darkness again, but now her eyes blazed with that same light, pulling me closer and closer...

"Captain!" A familiar voice drifted from far away, hazy in the ether of my thoughts. The three heads dipped beneath the water.

I stared after them. The warm, inviting feeling lingered, like waking from a pleasant dream. Slowly, my eyes and head cleared. Everything looked normal—river, forest, Lucky Seven.

Except I was now perched on the rail, with both my legs hanging over the water. The only thing that kept me from sliding right into the river was rough hands gripping my armpits. I didn't remember stepping over the edge of the boat.

Those hands pulled me back onto the deck, the shock of true waking like a bucket of cold water, and I saw Stock and Phan standing over me.

"What were you doing?" Stock asked.

I shook my head. "I...I thought I saw something in the water."

I checked my watch. 0358. What? I had only been talking to those girls for a few minutes.

Stock and Phan exchanged a look.

I sat up. "You know something about it?"

Stock scratched the back of his neck. "Well, Cap, an old lady said something in the village today. I didn't report it because it didn't seem like anything. She said the village is protected by..." He looked at Phan. "What's it called again?"

"*Mỹ nhân ngư.*"

That was the word the girl had shouted to Phan from the riverbank yesterday.

"What's that mean?" I asked.

"I don't know in English." Phan pointed at the river. "Live in water."

By now, Sukey and Dineen had joined us.

"Why didn't you tell me this before, Stock?"

Stock shrugged. "A folk tale didn't seem worth mentioning. It's got nothing to do with 288." He cleared his throat. "So, what exactly did you see out there?"

And suddenly, I wasn't sure. Had I really seen fish tails on those girls? Had they been girls at all? Had there been a light? This was the third night in a row I'd barely slept. I had never fallen asleep on watch before. I never would have tolerated it from my crew, but I found myself hoping that's what had happened.

But one detail felt too real to have been a dream: that lantern jaw...

"Could've been otters," Sukey said at last. "They got some pretty big otters in the delta."

"Yeah," Dineen said. "This far in the delta, they probably got animals we never even heard of."

Stock grabbed an M-16. "Well, if there's something in this river, let's just clear a path."

He aimed over the boat's rail, but before he could pull the trigger, Phan leaped for him.

"No!" Phan grabbed the rifle barrel and yanked it down.

Stock jerked on it, but Phan wouldn't let go.

"Are you crazy?" Stock shouted.

"Don't shoot!" Phan said.

He held Stock's gaze so fiercely that Stock finally looked to me.

Do you bring harm?

"Put down the rifle, Stock," I said.

Only when Stock relaxed his grip on the weapon did Phan release it.

"Everyone stay calm," I said. I turned to Sukey. "How deep is this river?"

"The Mekong can run from a few feet to 300, depending," Sukey said. "Right here in this spot, I have no idea."

We shoved off once the sun brightened the eastern sky enough for us to see our way out. Stock pushed Lucky Seven as fast as he could through the grasping mangrove trees and the rest of us hung on all the way back to Đồng Tâm.

We debriefed with Captain Freeman as soon as we put in, and we kept it short and sweet: 288 sunk, no sign of Jackson or his crew. Freeman listed them as missing in action, and though he later organized land and aerial searches, no one found any trace of them.

In the meantime, the captain must have sensed how shaken we were because when the time came, he sent a different PBR to extract SEAL Team Two. I don't think I could have handled another trip into the delta.

I ran into a member of the SEAL team a couple of days after their return. He told me they never did see the VC force they were supposed to intercept. However, they did see something strange in the spot where the canal met the river.

"Sampans," he said. "A whole bunch, all capsized or sunk, and weapons scattered everywhere. They must have belonged to the gang we were looking for, but no sign of them at all. We were the only other force in the area. I don't know what could have happened to them."

"Me either," I said, even as I thought again of the word *mỹ nhân ngư*. I repeated it to myself often, even though I refused to look it up or ask any of the interpreters on the base what it meant.

ABOUT THE AUTHORS

Katia Combe is a Peruvian-American writer and literacy advocate descended from the Quechua people. She writes middle-grade and young adult fiction that explores identity, belonging, and the quiet power of ancestral memory.

She volunteers in her local writing community and works actively with Operation Literacy. Her mission is to help kids who look like her discover their voices through writing and fall in love with reading.

When she's not writing or championing literacy, Katia is a wife, mother to two spirited boys, and doggy mom to two very spoiled pups who think they run the house—and sometimes, they do.

Karen Dent's creative life began in NYC as an actress/playwright where she sold, "The Soaps: Scene Stealing Scenes" to Meriwether Publishing. She joined a filmmaking group and wrote, "The Bloated Beetle" which won first prize in Screamfest's Short Screenplay Film Festival. Moving to Massachusetts, she and her sister Roxanne, also a published author, collaborated on a one-act comedy that won a 'Newbie Award' for Best New One-Act Play at the Firehouse Theater in Newburyport. Focused on writing short fiction she's sold mysteries, sci-fi, paranormal, fantasy and horror to various publications. Karen is currently working on her first novel, "A Case to Murder For", a paranormal mystery inspired by her characters in, "A Case To Die For", which sold to an anthology by Ticonderoga Publications. Karen loves animals and is a member of the Berlin Group.

Ikechukwu Henry's writings tackle the issues of environmental and climatic crisis, mental health, queerness, family dynamics, and speculation of otherworldliness. He was "honourable mention" in 2025 Stanley Umezulike Crime Thriller Prize, fifth place in Speculative Christian Fiction Contest (2025) and won the Ma Keke Short Story Contest (2025). His works have appeared in numerous magazines including but not limited to Brittle Paper, The Kalahari Review, Lampblack Magazine, and others. When not writing, he could be found sourcing out latest magazines to submit.

McKel Jensen's work has appeared in multiple anthologies including the award-winning *In Spite of the Dark*. Her story "The Weeping Willow at Goblin Creek" won a Woolley award and appeared in the anthologies *Soul, Sand, & Sky* as well as *Utah's Best Poetry and Prose 2022*. McKel earned her Master of Arts degree from Weber State University and currently resides in Brigham City, Utah with her husband, three kids, one cat, and a dog.

Tim Keller is an avid reader who likes traveling, 80's music, and if the highway patrol is to be believed, driving way too fast. After working as a bouncer, mortgage researcher, computer repair technician, caregiver, and a brief, albeit disastrous, stint as a waiter in anachronistic drag, he decided he wanted to be a writer when he grew up. A keen observer of human nature, Tim enjoys writing stories about all kinds of people from all walks of life. His work can be found in various literary journals and anthologies, including *Mirrored Realities, In the Shimmering, Between Places*, and the *Helicon West Anthology*.

L.S. Kunz lives in Utah with her husband. She is a member of the League of Utah Writers and has received awards for her short stories and middle grade fiction, including the Utah Original Writing Competition and the Olive Woolley Burt Award. Her work has appeared in *Ellery Queen Mystery Magazine, The Last Line, Baubles From Bones, The Genre Society, Utah's Best Poetry & Prose* for 2023 and 2025, and *Winter Horrorland: An Undertaker Books Anthology*.

Jennifer Monsen grew up in a desert that was once Lake Bonneville. Jennifer works as a music therapist by day. By night she is an aspiring writer with a bent towards the strange and the fantastic. Her first love is storytelling in all its forms; her second love is pizza. Find her at https://jentellingstories.blogspot.com.

K.G. Montgomery is an award-winning author, and sometimes an unproductive day dreamer, who has published short stories in a variety of genres. Her stories can be found in published anthologies such as *Emergence, In Spite of the*

Dark, *Joyride*, *Metamorphosis*, *Spirals*, *'Tis the Season*, and more. Her novel, *Harding Proper*, was awarded the 2022 Gold Quill Award from the League of Utah Writers. In addition to writing, K.G. enjoys creating art, watching movies, and spending time with her family. She also declares that peach cobbler ice cream is the best flavor ever.

Vincent H. O'Neil is the Malice Award-winning author of the Exile mystery series from St. Martin's Press and the military science fiction Sim War series (written as Henry V. O'Neil) from HarperCollins. His Interlands horror series features a young historian named Angela "Ree" Morse, and it's set in Providence, Rhode island. His short stories have appeared in Mystery Tribune, Parsec, Bourbon Penn, Lovecraftiana, and other magazines. His website is www.vincenthoneil.com.

Shawn Pollock is the author of the novels *The Road to Freedom* and *The Cowboy Ninja Murders* (Book One in the Royal City Mysteries Series). His short stories have appeared in *Frontier Tales*, *Flash Fiction Magazine*, *Mysterical-E*, *We Are Dangerous: The League of Utah Writers 2023 Anthology*, *Cinnabar Moth Literary Collections*, and *Once Upon a Future Time Vol. 4*. Mystery is his favorite genre. He is an active participant in the League of Utah Writers Just Write chapter, writes in the evenings when time and energy allow, and has several stories in various stages of completion. Follow him on Facebook at @authorshawnpollock.

Edmond A Porter is an award-winning author from

Tremonton, Utah, whose creative journey began in personal nonfiction, chronicling lived experiences with quiet clarity.

Over time, his exploration of form has expanded to include fiction, flash fiction, and poetry, with his work appearing in three anthologies, two newsletters, and online magazines. He has also published a collection of personal essays. In his first foray into magical realism, Edmond explores the use of symbolism to illuminate the blurred thresholds between myth, memory, and cultural legacy. He is currently developing two rural historical fiction novels that examine the emotional texture of small-town life and the moral complexities that arise when progress meets tradition.

David Rodeback's two collections of short fiction won Silver and Bronze Quill awards in 2024 and were named Notable Reads in General Fiction by the 2025 Utah Book Awards. He lives in American Fork, Utah, works in West Valley City, and is the League of Utah Writers' 2025 Writer of the Year. He writes a contemporary Christmas story as a gift for his mother-in-law every year. He has yet to see Italy, he doesn't wear a black stone crucifix, and he has never knowingly put his blood in the sauce.

From *Pan's Labyrinth* to *Aliens* to *Star Wars* to *Blood Meridian*, **TJ Tarbet** has always been a fan of the harrowing, the mind-bending, and the fantastical. Now he writes science fiction and horror, often mixing the two as best he can.

Andrea Tillmanns lives in Germany and works full-time as a university lecturer. She has been writing poetry, short stories and novels in various genres for many years. Her poems and stories have been published in The World of Myth, Hawthorn & Ash (Iron Faerie Publishing), SciFanSat, and other journals and anthologies. She has also published more than twenty books in German. More information about the author and her texts can be found on her website www.andreatillmanns.de

E.B. Wheeler is the author of over a dozen books of history, historical fiction, and historical fantasy, including Whitney Award finalists *Born to Treason* and *A Proper Dragon* and Whitney Award winner *Cruel Magic*, as well as several short stories, magazine articles, and scripts for educational software programs. She earned a B.A. in history with an English minor from BYU and graduate degrees in history and landscape architecture from Utah State University. In addition to writing, she sometimes consults about historic preservation and teaches history, and she loves gardening, folk music, reading, and traveling with her husband and kids.

www.ingramcontent.com/pod-product-compliance
Lightning Source LLC
Chambersburg PA
CBHW070823180626
46818CB00001B/372